WINTER TALES

Four Seasons Series
Book Three

WINTER TALES

a short story collection

Four Seasons Series
Book Three

by

Bruce K Beck

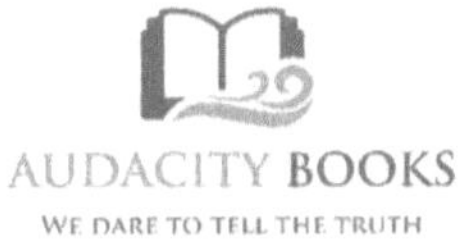

AUDACITY BOOKS

WE DARE TO TELL THE TRUTH

New York

This is a work of fiction. Names, characters, businesses, places, events, and incidents are either the products of the author's imagination or used in a fictitious manner.

ISBN 978-1-952031-24-3

This is a first edition from Audacity Books.
Please visit us on the web at www.audacitybooks.com.
For information about rights or purchases,
please email us at info@audacitybooks.com.

Contents

Foreword

Welcome to WINTER TALES, Book Three of Bruce K Beck's **Four Seasons Series** of short story collections. Readers get to revisit the seven sets of handsome couples they first met in summer and grew to love even more deeply in autumn. Seven sets of narrators and the people who love them as they navigate their lives in the winter wonderland that is New York City.

Welcome to new twists, dreams that seem to be falling into place as well as dreams that seem out of reach, deepening passions, surprises of various sorts, and family obligations, of course. Seven different takes on life and love as the Big City provides the perfect, frosty background.

Look for SPRING TALES, coming soon from Bruce K Beck and Audacity Books.

New York City, October 1, 2023

This book is dedicated to those, like me,
who love New York City in all seasons.

The voicemail turned up on my phone halfway between Christmas and New Year's—that strange week that always promises to be so festive and then turns out to be mostly about drinking too much champagne plus getting less sleep than intended. It seemed odd to hear Nancy's voice again. We hadn't really spoken since our high school graduation. And yet, she was now Tommy's soon-to-be-ex-wife.

Her message was short and to the point: She wanted to talk to me. I returned her call the following afternoon. "Hi, Brian," she said. "Thanks for getting back to me. I wanted you to know that Melissa will be in New York for a few days in mid-February. One of her classmates at Georgetown has an aunt who lives in Rome and teaches at the American School. She offered to put the girls up for a week. It's their winter break. I think the trip is a good idea—better than skiing somewhere—and it will help Melissa practice her Italian."

"Wow!" I said. "I only saw her the one time, when she was about four. And now she's all grown up. It hardly seems possible."

"Tell me," Nancy said. "Yes, all grown up and sharp as a whip. And she looks so much like Tom it's uncanny. It sits on her well. You'll see what a beauty she is. I hope. Anyway, I told her she could go to Rome as long as she stops in New York to see her dad first. I don't want them estranged."

"No," I said. "Neither do I."

"I'm not avoiding Tom," she said. "I'll email him tomorrow. But I wanted to talk to you first, Brian. I'm hoping you'll let Melissa stay in your apartment."

"Of course," I said. "And it's Tommy's home, too."

"I think she'll get over her anger if she spends some time with Tom. And with you, of course." I knew that couldn't have been an easy thing to say.

"Tommy will be thrilled," I said. "And so am I." That was also a little less than easy to say. But I said it. And I said it with an open heart.

"I'll text you the dates," Nancy said. "You know, Brian has quite fallen in love with you," she said of their son—hers and Tommy's. "It seems to be a family trait." There was an icy silence. But a brief one. "Sorry, Brian," Nancy said. "That was an attempt at levity. Thank you for doing this. And thank you for taking good care of Tom." Talk about words that are not easy to say!

It had been an interesting autumn, with son Brian's decision to come for a visit in October. The air was cleared, I supposed. I had assumed that we wouldn't see him again for quite a while. But then he asked us to billet him and his schoolmate Jeremy for a few days before Christmas. I had been nearly as smitten with Brian as I had been with his father when we were both about five. I was delighted at the prospect of seeing son Brian again so soon.

Of course, I knew that the college boys only wanted a place to stay while they explored New York on their holiday recess. Three days, and they would head south to spend Christmas with Nancy's family.

But I welcomed them into our home just as warmly as if they had come to visit Tommy and me—rather than the greatest city on Earth. I vowed to give them all the freedom they needed and whatever else I could offer to make their stay a happy one.

Predictably, we didn't see all that much of Brian and Jeremy while they were in town. One dinner—which Tommy cooked—and some comings and goings. I did notice the intensity of their bond, and I guessed that Brian was right when he had told me, in October, that he hoped he and Jeremy would be friends for life. They deserved it. Everyone deserves a friendship like that.

I was maybe feeling a little teary when they were preparing to leave for Penn Station and an evening train to Baltimore. I went to the kitchen to retrieve the sandwiches and beverages we had assembled for them. Brian followed me. As I was reaching into the fridge, he said, "Thank you, Bri."

"Your dad and I loved having you here," I said. "I hope you know that."

"Look, Bri," he said, "I should have told you before. But I didn't. So, I'll tell you now: I'm proud that Dad has you as his mate. And I love you nearly as much as he does." I'd have melted into a great puddle on the kitchen floor, of course, had it been possible. Instead, I reached for Brian and held him as close to my heart as I could manage.

Then I slapped him on the butt and said, "Out of here, young man! You have a train to catch. And I'd prefer not to have an audience when I fall apart in my own kitchen!"

Tommy was delighted with the news of Melissa's visit, of course. He had carried so much guilt since his bust-up with Nancy. Not that it hadn't been years in the making. Two decades, to be exact. But there was no point in pursuing what-ifs. What if Tommy had never told me, right after graduation, that he had to end our friendship because he couldn't return my feelings? What if we had run away together at age eighteen and created a universe of our own? And, of course, what if Tommy hadn't married a fine young woman and co-created two exquisite children?

I lived, mostly, in the real world. And so did Tommy—especially since June. His decision to leave Nancy and declare his love for me had seemed shocking, I'll admit. But the months since then had been so easy. So full of joy. So complete, I suppose. Spending every night with Tommy in my bed was like a sweet dream. And making love nearly every day— yes, we were still in that stage of our lives together— felt more like a fantasy than the blood, sweat, and tears that had forged it. And here we were celebrating our first adult Christmas together. I hardly noticed, having lived in a holiday wonderland for months. I needed nothing more than Tommy in my arms to fill my heart with celebration.

"You're being great about this, Bri," he said. "It can't be easy for you, having another Whitaker in the house."

"Don't be silly, Tom Cat," I said. "Your daughter belongs here, with her old man."

"*Our* daughter," he said. It was a jagged thought, but Tommy's kiss smoothed over the rough edges. "Melissa is remarkable, if I do say so myself. Thanks to Nancy, no doubt. I didn't do that much hands-on parenting—the way fathers do these days—but I tried to stay present in their lives. Melissa had a big crush on her dad from the day she was born. I guess I thought she would always be Daddy's girl and that I could do no wrong." Tommy grew silent as the weight of reality settled onto his shoulders.

February seemed a long way off. I tried to concentrate on the days at hand. "Jenna wants us at her apartment about 10:00 on Tuesday. I told her we'd bring caviar. Salmon roe, I think. Sturgeon prices are astronomical. Will you make some blini that Jenna can warm up a little? I'll get some lemons and sour cream and extra butter. And a red onion."

"Of course, Bri Baby. I'm glad we're going to welcome in the new year, quietly, with Jenna."

"And then we can walk home, if need be," I said, "since there is *never* a free cab in Manhattan after midnight on New Year's Eve. I don't even want to know what the Uber holiday surcharge is going to be."

"We'll be fine," Tommy said. "Even if there's a blizzard. You've kept me warm for most of my life, Bri, both in person and in memory all those years we were apart." That earned him a deep kiss. "And besides," he said, "my new Christmas parka is warm enough for both of us." I had been delighted when I spied it while Christmas shopping—at Saks, of all places. I liked the way the coat said practical warmth and elegance at the same time. Not an easy task for a down parka.

"I'm glad you like the coat, Tom Cat," I said. But mostly I was glad that he had decided, in the spring, that we should join our lives—as adults this time—and make up for all the years apart since high school. I knew it wasn't easy for him to give up his marriage and risk alienating his two children. I would never have encouraged him had it not felt so right.

I hadn't been idle for the two decades since high school, of course. I had built a career, of sorts, and one LTR, anyway. I think ten years is worth calling long term. Freddy is among the most attractive men I've ever met. And he loves me. Not enough, as it turned out, but his love is genuine. I never doubted that. Unfortunately, I learned that I couldn't rely on it. But I formed another relationship that has buoyed me through all the ups and downs.

Jenna Lazlo is a remarkable woman, and I've felt privileged to have her friendship. We first started working together early on in my decade with Freddy. So, Jenna first knew me when I was buoyant and loving and optimistic about the future. Freddy's warmth and sexuality had convinced me *we* had a future. When it turned out that Fred's warmth and sexuality had been refocused on another man—a boy, really, I always thought—Jenna was there to catch me as I fell to Earth.

Jenna has had some heartaches of her own over the course of our friendship. I hope I've been a good and loyal friend. I've done my best. When Jenna and Tommy bonded—over shared humanity as much as over shared love for me—I counted myself blessed. Yes, New Year's Eve with Jenna. Perfect. "And then, can we spend New Year's Day in bed?" I asked Tommy.

"We can do whatever makes my Bri Baby happy," he said. Yes. Happiness. Tommy had brought me that. And it seemed so effortless for him. For me,

too, of course. And yet, I can't say I felt really secure.
Too many things could go wrong. Couldn't they?

I've always loved January in New York. The whole
month seems calm, as if we are snowed in—or nearly
so—every day. Jenna and I made it to work most
days and accomplished some good, here and there,
for the deserving organizations that needed funding.
Tommy started his studies for the New York State
bar exam, as he had promised. I never questioned
his career decisions. Tommy had told me in the fall
that he had enough money to live on and that he
wanted to honeymoon until Christmas. How could I
argue?

Otherwise, life was about having a good dinner
and making love. Perfect. And then came February.
I was only just a little bit nervous about Melissa's
visit. Tommy seemed fine with it. I tried to take my
cues from him, since I had no real experience of his
younger child. "Here's another Whitaker for you,
Bri," Tommy said when his daughter arrived at our
apartment. "Melissa, meet the original Brian. And
this must be Emma."

We welcomed them into our home. I grabbed two
suitcases, and we showed the girls to the office/extra
bedroom. Nancy had been right, of course: Melissa
was drop-dead gorgeous and so much like her dad
that it was a bit shocking. Unfortunately, the Ice
Princess veneer she had imposed upon herself was
most unattractive. I would have been happy to accept her displeasure all for my own, had she spared

Tommy. But she seemed determined to chill both of us.

Melissa's friend Emma, however, was much warmer—and kinder, I suspected. "Let us know if you need anything," I said. "We'll be in the living room having a nightcap. Feel free to join us if you want to. Otherwise, I suppose we'll see you in the morning." I couldn't think of anything else to say, so I left the room. The frost between Tommy and his daughter chilled my heart. And it was oddly alienating, as if I had no participation in the situation.

In the days that followed, I won't say that Melissa paced the apartment like a caged tigress. But she always had an air of "I'm only doing this because Mom insisted." She mostly ignored me. I'd have been fine with that had she been a little warmer with Tommy. No such luck.

And then Emma got the text from her aunt—from her aunt's nurse, really—explaining that she had come down with some mysterious flu that had left her hospitalized. And so the visit to Rome was off. Emma was a good sport about it. She seemed even-tempered about everything. Melissa seemed *wounded* by the news, as if the universe had planned some negativity just for her. Tommy and I gritted our teeth and tried to figure out how to make the situation work.

At lunch that Thursday, Jenna said, "Bri, why don't you all come for dinner tomorrow night? I'll make something that *isn't* Italian, so we can get Melissa's mind off Rome. I'll call Tommy and see what he wants to bring. Lebanese, I think. Everyone loves *mezze*." It was generous of Jenna to offer her help. I was grateful, but not entirely comfortable with the idea.

Melissa spooked me, just a little. There, I've said it. She seemed a bit unpredictable. I couldn't have cared less, really, what she said or did to me. I'm not fragile. Nor are my loved ones. But I felt a certain responsibility to keep both Tommy and Jenna safe. 'Safety' and 'Melissa' rarely appeared together in the same thought.

Jenna welcomed the four of us into her home that Friday evening. So far so good. Tommy had stuffed some grape leaves with rice and a little ground lamb. They were the warm kind, served with broth and yogurt. Perfect winter fare. Jenna had made all sorts of spreads—including my favorite eggplant one—and a roasted chicken with onions and sumac.

That dish reminded me of something a Jordanian gym buddy had served me a few years before. He called it Circassian chicken because his family was originally from the north—the Caucasus. Jenna said her version was Palestinian. I'm always more interested in flavor than ethnicity. And the table was laden with flavorful dishes. The wine was good. The company was good—for the most part. I began to relax. It occurred to me later that I might have let my guard down too soon. I don't suppose we ever know enough about what might happen next.

As Jenna and I were clearing the dinner things and setting out the desserts, Melissa said something to Jenna so shocking that I've never been able to remember the exact words. It must have been something like, "How come these two men are your best friends?" Without actually saying it, Melissa managed to ask Jenna why she was a fag hag. There was an implication of "old maid," too, I think. Jenna seemed more surprised than wounded. I was horrified.

Tommy sprang to his feet. "Look, Missy. You can be as snarky as you like with me. I've probably earned it. But Jenna is your host, and I won't allow you to be disrespectful to her. Get your coat. We're leaving. You're no longer welcome here." Melissa froze. I bit my lip. Emma glazed over in the way we all probably do when a family feud breaks out and the family is not ours. "Now," Tommy said quietly but firmly. Melissa did as she was told.

When Emma rose to get her coat, too, I took her arm and indicated that she should remain. And so, there were still three of us at table when Tommy and Melissa left Jenna's apartment. I finally broke the ice: "Well, Emma," I said, "aren't families fun!"

"No need to go there," Emma said. "I have a family of my own. I just wish Lissa could let go of her anger. I had to. When my parents divorced. It wasn't easy."

"No, I'm sure it wasn't," Jenna said. "But you got through it. And so you've earned a taste of the best baklava in New York City." Jenna busied herself with assembling dessert plates and pouring coffee for the three of us. The storm had passed. More or less. We finished dinner two shy of the original guest count. I was happy to remain at Jenna's for a while. It meant that I could avoid—or delay my involvement in—the storm that was surely brewing at home.

As Emma and I were leaving, Jenna handed me a little white bakery box to take to Melissa. "She needs all the sweetness she can get," Jenna said. No argument there. The trip home, with Emma, was a bit foggy. I had high hopes for a reconciliation between Tommy and his daughter but not much encouragement from their recent encounter. Emma was quiet. I was not much up to chitchat myself.

When I let us into the apartment, Tommy and Melissa seemed to be at a standoff. "Good timing," Tommy said. "I think Brian has a right to hear what I'm about to say. And so does Emma, for that matter." We hung our coats and I headed for the kitchen to pour myself a brandy. Emma decided on ginger ale. We returned to the living room with our beverages and settled in quietly.

Tommy said to his daughter, "This is how life works: If you want to be welcome, you have to behave yourself. No, you have to be worthy. I don't give a flying fuck about good manners. I want you to care about the people around you. And if you can't do that, then forget about having a real life. I'm not going to apologize to you, daughter, for my choices. But I can wish you the same joy I felt the day you were born, and the same joy I feel every moment I'm with Brian. Some of it's earned, but most of it is serendipity. You get to decide how much joy you're willing to accept. So, it really is all about you, Missy. But not the way you thought. The world owes you nothing, but it offers you infinite possibilities. Which ones will you choose?"

Melissa looked defiant, but less so than before her dad called her on her behavior. I left the room without comment to head to the kitchen and add another splash of brandy to my glass. When I returned, Emma had gone to the spare bedroom, and Tommy and Melissa still seemed at cross purposes. "If you can't be civil," Tommy continued, "then maybe you can take your anger to a hotel room. I don't think your mother would be very pleased, but I can always make a reservation and book an Uber. It's up to you."

I searched for a way to smooth things over. "No one's going anywhere tonight," I said. It was not a declaration, but rather a suggestion, really. "Let's talk about this tomorrow." Melissa picked up her very expensive coat from where she had tossed it when she and Tommy got home. She shot me a glance that was decidedly cool, and then she headed to "her" room.

I took Tommy by the hand and said, as softly as I could manage, "Come to bed, darling." When we had brushed our teeth and slipped into bed, I said, "Let her go, Tommy. She'll come back to you. She can't help herself. She adores you. She'll get over me. Or not. Doesn't matter. You two have an unbreakable bond. That's what counts."

"But what about us, Bri?" he asked me. "The bond that you and I share is the most precious thing to me."

"We're fine, my love," I said. "We can handle anything." And I believed it, as I cradled Tommy in my arms. I pulled the comforter up tightly around us, as if goose down could form a protective barrier against the hurts of the world.

"Bri to the rescue," Tommy said. "This makes me feel like I'm twelve years old again. And you're soothing me—after Dad just beat the shit out of me. Again. I wouldn't have survived childhood without you, Bri."

"Hush, Tommy," I said. "You need some rest. I'll hold you all night if you'll let me." Tommy snuggled in, resting his head on my chest. My man of steel—my perfect Southern gentleman—needed me. And I began to weep, softly. When Tommy's breathing re-laxed into the regular rhythm of sleep, I joined him.

Nancy's phone call was not particularly welcome, but it did seem inevitable. I answered. "Sorry, Brian," she said, "I didn't think Melissa would be in New York long enough to be such a pain. Tom wants to put them up in a hotel. I want the girls to spend the rest of their break with me. But what do you want?" What, indeed?

"I think they should stay put," I said. "I think Melissa should have the time to blow off steam—or frost, in her case—and get over herself. I don't want her to leave until she and Tommy come to terms." There. I said it.

Nancy was silent for a bit. And then she said, "Brian, let's try it your way." And so that's how we started the next week. I was mostly at the office dur-ing business hours, so that took me out of Storm Central for big chunks of the day. I was glad that Tommy and Melissa would have so much forced face time. They were so very much alike—in some ways—and yet so locked into their status as adversaries.

I was aware that poor Emma had found herself in an unpleasant situation not of her own making. I took her to dinner on Tuesday night. To my favorite Thai. "So tell me about you," I said, as we filled let-tuce leaves with chicken *larb* and basil leaves and some fresh herb I had never encountered and rolled our own Thai tacos.

"Oh, I'm drifting a little this term," she said. "Last year I was certain I wanted to be a psychiatric social worker. Right now, I'm thinking business administration is my calling. Something to do with the arts, maybe. I could see myself guiding a dance troupe, or maybe a small museum somewhere."

"Yes!" I said enthusiastically. "I can see that, too. I've worked for non-profits so long that I can spot a kindred soul. Yes, I think you'll love it. Jenna and I both will be happy to offer you any help you might need. And what about Melissa?" And then we both started to laugh.

"Melissa is ... Melissa," Emma said. "She would never admit it to you, Brian, but what she wants most is to save starving babies in Africa. And she'd be good at it, too."

"Indeed," I said. "If she approached me for a grant, I'd say, 'Yes, Ms. Whitaker. How much do you need?'" That earned another round of laughter. But it was a softer kind of mirth, tempered by shared experience. "If only she and Tommy could ... I know they're both hurting from this rift, and I don't know what I can do to help."

"I guess it's up to them, Brian," she said. "I told Melissa months ago that I think her expectations for her parents are unrealistic. Happily Ever After is different for everybody. I had to learn that. I'm not sure why she hasn't."

"You're not from the South, are you?"

"No. Missouri," Emma said.

"Well, where we grew up and Tommy raised his family, near Baltimore," I said, "there are certain expectations. I can't really explain it. If I had understood it better when I was a child, I would have maybe fit in better. It's not Mom and apple pie, exactly. And it's not devotion to the Confederacy (although that is very much in existence). It's more about a code of behavior for Southern ladies and gentlemen. Tom crossed a line when he fell in love with me. Too much information?"

"No, not at all, Brian. Actually, I have a gay uncle who might have been considered the black sheep of the family. But he was also the most charming sheep in the family. And everybody knew it. My parents were ex-Hippies, so they didn't judge. Much. My Uncle Jerry gave me a charm for my birthday a few years ago. I've worn it every day since." Emma showed me the little gold heart she wore on a delicate chain around her neck.

"So, how's your Uncle Jerry doing?" I asked, even though I had no right to ask anything about Emma's family.

"He's doing great, actually," she said. "He and his husband moved to Phoenix and started an energy business. Solar, wind, I think they're working all the renewables."

"Excellent," I said. We finished our dinner on a positive note. But then it was back to the apartment and the permafrost that had taken it over. Unlike the polar ice caps, there was no evidence of a thaw in that particular part of the environment. It was that evening, just as Tommy and I were preparing for bed, that I became restless for a solution to the problem at hand. Surely it showed no signs of solving itself.

Hmmm ... Bri to the rescue, I thought. Why not? Why couldn't I be the one to bridge the gap? I was an interested party, after all. Not the cause of the father-daughter rift, exactly, but a factor, nonetheless. Who better to mend fences than one who helped to topple them? Yes, but how would I achieve this feat of diplomacy? I slipped into Scarlett O'Hara mode and decided, *No, I won't think about that now. I'll think about it tomorrow.*

Naturally, I asked Jenna for her help. What did I know about nineteen-year-old young women, after all? What did I know about anything? "I know you'll be respectful of Melissa's autonomy, Brian," Jenna said. "That's important. But don't be afraid to flirt a little. She definitely responds to the male. Even the bullest dykes I've known have a soft spot for Daddy. And you're the closest male to her one and only dad. That gives you power, Brian, no matter how much she might resent it. Don't think she doesn't also resent her mother for having been the "other woman" when she was vying for Daddy's affection when she was growing up. It's complicated."

Indeed. "Okay," I said. "I'm maybe going into this battle with insufficient understanding of the enemy, but I can make up for that with determination. I just have to get the two of us together. Melissa doesn't like me very much, in case you didn't notice."

"She doesn't like much of anybody at the moment, Bri. Not even herself. But don't let that stop you," Jenna said. Indeed. I set out to concoct a situation to get Tommy and Emma out of the house so that Melissa and I could be alone together. I texted Tommy and suggested that he choose a movie for him and Emma to see. He agreed. It would all be quick and casual, and the two of them would be out of the apartment before Melissa realized what was happening. Or so I hoped.

Melissa isn't stupid, of course, so she was about to retire to "her" room for the night when I told her I had ordered a pizza—from the best pizzeria in the neighborhood. "I'm not hungry," Melissa said. The house phone rang to announce that the pizza was on its way up.

"Well, you'd better eat anyway," I said, "because you'll be hungry later and there won't be any food." Melissa tossed her glossy mane, pouted slightly, and sat at my dining table. I received the delivery and unpacked the pizza and salad. We ate. She accepted a little red wine. I accepted a lot. We were silent to start. Melissa seemed—subdued, I suppose. For her, anyway. And she remained silent. It seemed I would have to break the ice.

"What do you think of New York so far?" I asked.

"It's okay," she answered. "I'm not sure what I was expecting."

"Why are you so angry?" I asked. That earned me nothing more than an angry look. "I know a little bit about anger," I said. "I'll tell you what I know." Melissa seemed unimpressed, as usual. I continued: "When your father and I were eighteen, he told me he had to end our friendship—because he couldn't return my feelings. I knew that was bullshit. I knew he loved me just as much as I loved him—and had, since we were kids. Did that make me angry?" Melissa chewed her pizza, almost thoughtfully, it seemed.

"I never got angry at your dad," I said. "Not then. I knew exactly how much his decision hurt him, because I could compare it to the pain in my heart. In case you don't understand, your dad made his choice because he also loved your mother, and because he wanted to be a dutiful member of his family, and because he wanted children, by the way. And that wish came true for him in spades. No parent could ask for finer offspring than you and your brother. I'm giving you the benefit of the doubt here, Melissa, because I see some potential." That earned me a deserved smirk.

I was starting to feel way out of my depth, but there was no turning back. "I promised to talk about anger," I said. "When I had finished college and started a real job—when I was maybe twenty-five—I met a nice guy named Fred. You'd fall in love with him, too, Melissa. Everyone does. Freddy and I started living together. And that was when the anger set in. Not because the relationship was a disappointment to me—far from it—but because my life with Freddy showed me what your dad and I could have shared."

I hadn't really gone there in my mind for some years. For good reasons. "When the anger came, it was white-hot. Anger at life, anger at Baltimore, and, yes, anger at your dad. It took me years to let go of it. I don't recommend holding onto anger. It's bad for the complexion."

"But how could he do this to our family?" Melissa asked.

"We have a lot in common, you and I," I said. Melissa looked doubtful. "You make your father very unhappy, and that makes *me* very unhappy. I don't much care what you think of me—or if you think of me at all. And if you were not Tom's daughter, I doubt I'd waste a thought on you. Other than beauty and a hardness most Southern women try to hide, you don't show me much. I choose my friends based on the content of their hearts. And if I met you casually, with no ties, I would assume that yours is deficient. Just saying."

I instantly regretted going in that direction, but it was done. And just like a boiled egg, it could not be undone. "Let me tell you something about your father you may not know." I was scrambling for direction, but Melissa seemed to soften a little. "Did you know *his* father?" I asked.

"Not really," she answered. "He died just after my fourth birthday. My Pawpaw was tall and handsome, and he used to bounce me on his knee and kiss the top of my head. That's about all I remember of him."

"Well, he was tall and handsome, for sure. And charming, in a Southern sort of way. But there was another side to him as well. He used to beat your father. Did you know that? And your grandmother, too. He was very good at delivering blows that wouldn't show."

"I don't think I want to hear this, Brian," Melissa said.

"Too real for you?" I asked. "Well, you don't need to ask your father or your grandmother about it. They're both well out of that nightmare. But I was there, too. Sometimes. Afterward. On the edge of things. So, I can tell you I used to put salve on your dad's welts and help him into his pajamas so he could get some sleep." Melissa was silent. I wasn't quite ready to let go of the topic. I continued: "Your grandfather seemed to dote on his daughter, though. Even then I wondered if their relationship was entirely healthy. Ask your Aunt Kate. It's none of my business."

Melissa squirmed. We finished our pizza and salad in silence. I would have loved to end the conversation, but it seemed unfinished. "So, you're asking how your father could do this to you and your family—how he could fall in love with me? At some point, you'll have to forgive him for not being exactly the man you wanted him to be. And you'll probably have to forgive me for being the person who holds a big chunk of your father's heart. Fortunately, his heart is big enough to also hold you and Brian and your mother with no strain on its capacity. I'm not your competition, Melissa, and I'm unwilling to be the villain in this piece. I've loved your father with my whole heart since I was five years old. And I've had to do without him for half my life. I'm not willing to return there. And neither is he."

When I was satisfied that Melissa had gotten the message—to some degree, anyway—I got up and made coffee. I also unboxed the little raspberry tart I had purchased on my way home from work. I sliced it in half and plated the two halves, returning to the dining table with the sweets and a fresh pot of coffee. "Look, you don't have to take my word for any of this," I said. "Ask your dad how he feels. He'll tell you."

"Mom said you wanted Emma and me to stay here with you this week. Why?" Melissa asked.

"Because you're Tom's daughter, and because Emma is a charming young woman who is good company. Why else?" I answered. That earned me a smile, of sorts. The first one of the visit? Perhaps.

"I'm not sure I know how to handle this."

"Join the club," I said.

"I never thought my father would run off with another man," Melissa said. I shot her a look that was designed to nip that flower in the bud. We finished our dessert and coffee in silence.

"Look, Melissa," I said. "You don't have to like me, but your father's happiness is the most important thing in my life. I'm thinking there must be a way for us to play on the same team."

"Brian, I think maybe I *do* like you," Melissa said.

"Really, why?" I asked.

"Because you're smart and funny and good-looking and kind, sometimes, and—I'm still working on this—because Dad loves you. Mom loves you too, Brian, did you know that?"

"Bullshit!"

"No, it's true. She told me. This morning. On the phone. She said if you had asked her to marry you, she'd have accepted. And when you didn't seem headed in that direction, she was happy to accept Dad. Because he has most of your good qualities..."

"Plus lots of family money," I suggested. "He was quite a catch."

"Yes, but that was the least of it. Mom doesn't have to worry about things like that, Brian. She liked the idea of being Mrs. Whitaker, of course. And she liked Dad. So, she accepted him. And Dad is better-looking than you are, Brian. You'll have to admit that."

"Freely." We were silent for a bit. And then I said, "Well, I've turned into a grumpy old thing, as you well know. But I could probably learn to like you, too." So when Tommy and Emma got home from their movie, Melissa and I were sitting quietly while Melissa watched something she had found on Netflix and I sipped a brandy—well-earned, I thought.

"We should think of something interesting to do this weekend, before you leave," Tommy said to the girls as we were all heading in the direction of bedtime. "The Statue of Liberty, or museums, or a corned beef sandwich at Katz's, or, what do you think?" They didn't seem all that interested in another New York adventure.

So I jumped in: "I thought maybe we could have lunch at Serendipity and then maybe see what's playing at the Music Hall."

Melissa said, "Brian, let's try it your way."

Our first Christmas together was like a fairy-tale holiday. Noah's cheeks were rosy, and his eyes sparkled with love and contentment. Or at least that was what I hoped I saw. We both had the week between Christmas and New Year's free, and that time together was the most precious gift we could have received.

"Toby, can we just spend the week in bed?" he asked me.

"That was my plan, Noah," I answered.

"I had one idea, though, Toby. It might require getting out of bed a time or two."

I wrapped my arms around his beautiful shoulders, kissed him deeply, and said, "Anything my perfect mate desires."

"Toby, you've taken so many pictures of me this year for so many clients, and yet I don't think there's a single picture of the two of us." It was true, of course. Since the first time Noah and I made love—in July—the mere sight of Noah's warm, creamy skin against the chocolatey smoothness of my own gave me an instant erection. Add his touch to the mix, and the results were orgasmic.

I had considered asking Noah if I could photograph us together. But I worried that it might seem a little pervy. And I didn't dare do anything that could spoil our happiness. So, I was relieved, that Christmas morning, as we emerged from clouds of Egyptian cotton and European white goose down, to hear my perfect lover ask for just what was on my mind.

It was a crystalline morning as I gazed out over Bryant Park. The skaters hadn't gotten underway yet, and the puffs of steam rising from street works were nearly the only movement outside. I said a prayer of gratitude—as I did most mornings—that my benefactor had not only taught me how to take pictures but had also given me a dream studio in which to take them.

It still seemed unbelievable that Lester had been able to buy the loft for a song—on a teacher's pay, with a little help from family money, most likely—the decade before I moved to New York. But the park behind the New York Public Library on Fifth Avenue had become Crack Central, to the detriment of property values all around it. On that quiet, cold Christmas morning, there was no longer any evidence of degradation.

The industrial-strength air system in my loft—*my* loft, was it really possible?—purred along almost imperceptibly, keeping Noah and me effortlessly comfortable as we slipped out of bed and into the kaftans my studio manager had just made for us. Unsurprisingly, they were perfect—fit, cut, fabric, color, finish. Noah's was a swirly blue that made him seem to shimmer like the night sky. Mine was a blend of green and royal purple that made me feel regal, indeed.

Over smoked salmon sandwiches I had bought the afternoon before, I said, "This coffee is fine, but it's never as good as Elijah's. I don't know how he does it. I'm going to give him a call now, to wish him a merry Christmas and to thank him for the kaftans. I could ask him if he's free—maybe Wednesday?—to help us with a photo shoot. What do you think?"

"Sure, Toby," Noah said. "Wednesday is fine. It doesn't matter to me when we do it." I kissed Noah deeply. It seemed to me that whether Noah had been drinking coffee or wine or nothing at all, and whether he had been eating a smoked salmon sandwich or a cheeseburger with onions or nothing at all, he always tasted like heaven. I feasted. He gave me everything I desired.

"Merry Christmas, Elly," I said when Elijah answered my call. "We love the robes. They're rather like you, Elijah. They're ... they're perfect, actually." I put him on speakerphone.

"Why, Mas'er Toby!" he said. "I's mighty pleased to hear dat. Dem little birds was powerful noisy whilst we was sewin', but I's guessin' it was worth it."

"You're a martyr, Elly," I said. "A Christian martyr."

"An' Mas'er Noah? I bet he be lookin' mighty fine." I snapped a picture of Noah on his phone and sent it to Elijah. "Ooooh, he done got celestial!" Elly said.

"Thanks, Elijah," Noah called out. "I owe you a big kiss."

"And when might I be able to collect my reward?" Elly asked.

"All right, my little friend," I said. "Could we get maybe almost serious for a moment?"

"I don't see why not," Elijah said. "Unless you're firing me. That's not appropriate for Christmas Day. Jes' ain't fittin'. 'Tain't fittin'."

"No, dear," I said. "Actually, I need to ask for your help. You can just say yes or no, without bowing to your African King."

"Yes. What do you need?"

"I want to take some pictures. With me in them. Pictures of Noah and me. I need some help setting them up. Can you give us a few hours on Wednesday afternoon? If we promise to take you to dinner?"

"Of course, Toby," Elijah said. "It would be my honor. What time do you want me?" So, that's how the shoot was arranged. And after that, Noah and I stripped off our beautiful new robes and went back to bed. The moment that Noah was in my arms again, I melted into our union.

One touch, and Noah always knew exactly what I needed of him. That Christmas morning—our first Christmas together—I needed to see how deeply I could fill his body. I needed to see if we could become one blended beast. I needed to own Noah and to *be* Noah, and for him to own Tobias and to *be* Tobias all at once. Tall order. But we did it.

When Noah and I had stirred a little from our post-ecstasy enervation, I began to untangle our limbs. Reluctantly. And then I said to him, as I fingered the soft sandy-colored hair at the base of his neck—or is it more like light auburn?—"Noah, you'll grow tired of me. I'm certain of it. And it will break my heart."

"Hush, Toby," he said. "How can you talk that way when we're just beginning to know each other? Every time I touch you; every time I taste your skin; every time I feel our bodies joined, I learn something new about you. Toby, I never thought I could love a man as much as I love you. Won't you just accept that, so we can get on with our lives?"

Noah had a point, of course. A valid point. I tried to be sensible—and cooperative. My efforts were interrupted by the jangling of my phone. Only Perry would dare to place a call on Christmas morning. I answered and put him on speakerphone:

"*Mele Kalikimaka*," I said. "How is my best friend this bright Christmas day?"

"Not as happy as you seem to be, but doing well," Perry said. "I wanted to thank you two for the bag."

"Not necessary."

"Nevertheless, I was touched," he said. Noah and I had decided to buy Perry a new valise from our favorite leather shop on Bleecker Street. It was large enough to hold a Chromebook and most of life's necessities, but small enough that it didn't scream "briefcase." It felt like butter, and it smelled like the back room in the hottest leather bar of your hottest leather bar fantasy.

"Do you really like it, Per?" I asked. "Because you can always return it—to us, I mean."

"I'll be proud to keep it, thank you very much," he said. "I hate to inject a little business into this holiday frivolity, but I need to schedule you two for a small swimwear shoot two weeks from today. I think we can squeeze it in, and the client understands that he needs to book earlier for their fall line, blah, blah, blah. You'll understand when you see who it is. Are you two okay with that?"

"Merry Christmas, Perry," Noah called. "Did you try on the other gifts?" While Noah and I were shopping in the Village, we also went to The Leather Man and bought Perry a jockstrap and a matching harness. His body had changed hardly at all since we had been lovers more than a decade before, so I knew the right size to get him, and I knew the features he would most enjoy.

Perry coughed a little and said, "No, not yet. But I'm sure they'll fit."

"I'm expecting a pic, Perry," Noah said. "Just a simple selfie will do. Nothing fancy." When we finished our call, Noah said to me, "Interesting, about Perry: He's a remarkably attractive man, but he doesn't seem to know it."

"I always thought that, too."

"He's the sort of man that, if you fell in love with him, then there'd be no turning back." I was startled by Noah's perception. Startled, and a little discomfited. I knew it was time for me to confess—beyond the *Reader's Digest* version of my history with Perry.

"We were classmates at Parson's. You know that," I said. "We fell into bed together the first week of our fall term. It was good. The sex was good. But no fireworks, as far as I was concerned. I don't know exactly what I expected. Maybe I had never met a nice guy before. Maybe sex and abuse were linked in my consciousness."

I really didn't want to go there, but I didn't know how to get out of it. It was my first Christmas with the first man I had ever felt complete, unconditional love for, and I guess I just wanted it to be sweet and uncomplicated. So much for that! Noah opened a bottle of chardonnay and poured two glasses. He didn't push me, but he also didn't let me off the hook.

"Noah, I've told you some things about my childhood," I said. "I've told you about the bully who used to humiliate me in his parents' garage. I probably didn't mention that while he had me on all fours on the concrete floor so he could pump me much too hard, he also shouted, 'Take that big white dick,

Nigger! It's too good for your sorry black ass, but take it, and tell me how grateful you are that I'm giving it to you.' And I did—both take it and thank him for it.

"And when Billy came inside me, he clung to me like I was his only lifeline. Because I was. Because Billy Bevins—the golden boy—was lost in a sea of doubt and despair. Because Billy Bevins loved me. I knew it. Even at age fourteen. I knew that when he clutched me and squirted his seed inside me it was because he needed me desperately."

I took a few minutes to breathe and sip my wine. And then I said, "Okay, I liked it when Billy fucked me. But I let him do it again and again because I was afraid, somehow, that he couldn't do without it—me. It was the *need* that kept me coming back to him. *His* need much more than mine. Does that make sense?"

"Perfect sense, Toby," Noah said.

"I broke it off, after high school graduation. I had to start a new life. Grandmaw told me Billy died suddenly about five years later. Some sort of freakish hunting accident. I knew better. I knew that he couldn't live with himself—because he couldn't live with me. Noah, I'm not sure how much more of this I have in me today. Fa-la-la-la-la and all."

"Hush, pumpkin," Noah said. "You don't have to do or say anything you don't want to. Until next week, of course, when we go back to work." I opened my arms, and Noah came to me and settled against my body. As always, the two of us were a perfect fit. I'd have been content to exist quietly—for the rest of my life, really—with Noah in my arms and nothing else to concern me. But it was talking about Perry that had gotten me started. And I needed to finish.

"So, about Perry," I said. "The truth is, I wanted to love him. But I couldn't do it because he was nothing like Billy. Perry is smart and kind and good-natured and wickedly funny sometimes. Nothing like Billy. I didn't know how to process that kind of man in my life.

"I knew that Perry liked the smell of leather, and that he wouldn't have minded if we had bought a flogger—the kind with the soft tails—to enhance our sex play. I had nothing against the idea of a little kink. But it all seemed too tame. It lacked—desperation. I shut down. I walked away from the chance to have a quality relationship with a quality man, because I had no idea how to do it.

"A few years later, when I had started to see Lester about once a week and Perry and I both were starting to focus on our careers, I realized that I had missed a great opportunity. Mostly, I realized that I loved Perry deeply. It seemed too late for the two of us. He was seeing a series of cute guys. I had my tame dates with Lester, plus I was fucking a series of cute guys I was more than happy to kick out of my bed as soon as rocks had gotten off.

"So when Perry said, 'Toby, I can make you a star if you'll let me manage you,' I said, 'Yes, Per, let's do it.' And the rest, as they say, is history." I wondered, of course, if I had been totally honest. I so wanted to give Noah that gift—the gift of utter transparency. I wanted to be the open book that Noah would choose to read again and again.

Noah came behind my chair and put his arms around me. We were silent for a while. The sweetness of his breath filled my senses. Elly's silks rustled ever so slightly at the tiniest movement. Noah's beautiful hands resting on my chest made me feel safe. Protected. Loved, I suppose. At last, Noah broke the silence:

"We're going to have to make some supper plans." True. We had been careless about holiday planning, because the prospect of some free time together had seemed entirely sufficient. We hadn't even bought gifts to exchange. We both sensed that our new love was gift enough, I think.

"I'll order in something easy," I said. "This is New York. Everything's open. How about falafels?"

"Perfect. Don't forget the hot sauce," Noah said. "You shared about your past, Toby. Could I?"

"Of course," I said. "I want to know everything about my man." Did I presume? Had I any right to think of Noah as mine? I couldn't be sure.

"When I was eight," Noah said, "I wanted to be a dancer. I don't know why, exactly, except that it seemed like such a challenge. It wasn't 'everything was beautiful at the ballet.' Nothing like that. I had nothing much at home to escape from, except boredom. You've been to Connecticut, Toby. You know what I mean."

"Indeed."

"I know there were Nureyev videos around. And Baryshnikov in his prime. They were thrilling to watch, but I think I just wanted to see what my body could do. I had no interest in football or baseball or basketball. I can play tennis, but so what? Now, dance—that looked dangerous! So, it was either dance or soccer. And dance won out. That sounds really lame, doesn't it?"

"No, Darling," I said. "It sounds like you were in touch with your body and with your feelings at an age when I was just flopping around wondering where the next wind would blow me. And usually it was a *boy* who wanted to blow me, rather than the wind."

Noah said, "I wish I had known you when you were a little boy, Toby. Thank you for introducing him to me today. I love him nearly as much as the man he grew into." That earned Noah a deep kiss, of course. I'm sure both of us would have been happy to continue that kiss in silence for the rest of the day—if not longer. But Noah had a story to tell, of course.

"I was a decent dance student. I never missed a class. My teacher praised my technique. But I knew, by age ten or twelve, that I didn't have the fire in the belly. And yet I kept getting better. So, whenever we had a recital, I danced Apollo or Prince Sigfried or Prince Albrecht or whatever cavalier was needed. And I was ... good. And so what?" Noah looked almost a little weepy. I poured him a splash of wine and waited.

"I nearly joined the school at ABT. I was accepted. My parents were concerned about me finishing school at home. I was undecided. And then came Christmas. I was maybe thirteen, nearly fourteen, I guess. My grandmother got tickets for the two of us to Alvin Ailey. We didn't go to the theater very often, so I was psyched.

"I don't remember all that much about the first two pieces except that they were exciting to watch and different from dance I was used to. And then came a solo: The most beautiful man I had ever seen—half naked, with skin the color of a Hershey bar—was alone on stage. It was pure theater: nothing but a body, movement, and some light. I'm sure there must have been music, but I have no memory of it. He danced. I was mesmerized. And when the dance climaxed, so did I!

"There I was, sitting in the balcony at City Center, next to my grandmother, and I had just creamed in my pants. So, by the time we got to "Revelations" I was a soggy mess. I decided that instead of putting on my jacket against the winter cold, I'd better hold it in front of my crotch. Somehow, I made it back to Connecticut."

I said, "I didn't think it was possible for me to love you any more than I did when we woke up this morning, Noah. But I do." We laughed a lot, and embraced a lot, and kissed a lot.

"Toby, there's a point to this story," Noah said, "beyond adolescent humiliation."

"Of course," I said.

"As Gramma and I were headed home, I realized that I had just witnessed dance performed by **dancers**. Especially the one whose performance had taken over my whole body and wrung the juice out of me. And at that moment, I realized—as if I needed confirmation—that I was merely a good athlete. Nothing more. In the weeks that followed, I finished out my commitments at the dance school. But I always felt like an impostor."

"Noah, you're the most honest man I know! And what other kid searches his soul like that?" I asked.

"Well, thanks, Toby," he said, "but that was a dark time for me. After years of thinking of myself as a dancer—sort of—I had to think of something else. Modeling seemed like a good idea. I knew I could do it, and I liked the idea of a career that could last for decades—as long as I don't get fat!

"The truth is, Toby, the first time I worked for you and Perry, I was excited about meeting you. I knew who you were, of course, and I had seen your pictures. But I was unprepared for the intensity of your smile when you welcomed me to this studio for the first time. And when the workday was over, I'd have been crushed if you hadn't asked me out to dinner."

"I'd have been crushed if you hadn't accepted."

"And then when we showered together and went to bed together, I knew, Toby. I knew that first night we were meant to be together. Even when you got scared and tried to push me away."

"You knew that was fear, didn't you?"

"I can smell it, Toby. I can smell it on myself! It's not a nice scent, is it?"

"No, it isn't. Noah, I'm glad you were patient with me."

"I didn't feel like I had a choice, Toby. I wanted you. And that was that. But I have to tell you, it wasn't until I was headed home the next day that I realized it was the Alvin Ailey soloist—in that holiday show at City Center when I was thirteen-going-on-fourteen—who prepared me for you."

"How so?"

"Because his art was so intense that it reached out into the audience and grabbed me by the balls. And I never experienced that sensation again until I met you."

"Noah, I have a creepy question to ask," I said. "I hope you can forgive me."

"Anything."

"Do you have a sexual preference for Black men?" I instantly regretted my question. I wondered if maybe I had just asked him if he likes BBC.

Noah considered my question for a moment, without seeming to judge the merit of it, and then he replied, "Toby, I have a sexual preference for men. I don't think I've ever judged their beauty or their quality or their value by their color. Why do you ask, Toby? Do you think I love you because you're a Black man?"

I was horrified, of course. I grabbed Noah and held him much too tightly, as if I feared he might escape my embrace and disappear into the starry Christmas night sky above us. And as long as he continued to wear Elly's new robe as camouflage, I might never find him.

"If I promise never to say stupid things like that again, will you really forgive me?" I asked him.

"Of course."

"Are you going to ask me if I have a preference for White boys? You have a right to ask that question."

"Do you, Toby—have a preference for White boys? Do you want me to ask you that question? Because it wouldn't occur to me to ask. But I will, if that's what you want. Toby, I'll do anything for you."

"I'm fucking this up royally," I said. "It's just that I adore you so totally, Noah, and I guess I wanted to be certain we understand each other completely. Maybe I hoped we could take race off the table. Maybe I'm just too stupid to live."

"Hush, Toby," Noah said. "Look, I'm trying to tell you that race doesn't interest me. I grew up in a very White part of Connecticut—which is firmly part of the USA, as I'm sure you've noticed—so I'll never be color-blind. But difference? It always felt like something to celebrate. Toby, could we put this topic to bed?"

"As long as we put ourselves to bed with it." And that's what we did. Just as the moon was starting to set, and just before I was about to drop off to sleep, I renewed my embrace of Noah's perfect body and said, softly, "By the way, Darling, I knew you were a dancer. Men don't develop an ass that beautiful any other way."

📖

"Okay, Boss. What are we doing?" Elijah asked me on Wednesday afternoon. Noah and I had talked things over before Elly arrived, so we were decided that we wanted some nude shots of the two of us in bed together, plus some shots of the two of us clothed. Chaste, but still romantic.

We wanted to make some memories and to make some images we could use for promotion—the sort of thing we could give to a "journalist" like Gabriela Simón. Gabby liked both of us, and she liked us to-gether—or so she told me. So, giving her quality portraits of us—exclusives, of course—could make all the difference in her press coverage of our work.

It seemed silly for a working photographer and a top model to be so concerned about image. But we worked in fashion, after all. So, image was every-thing. And our very livelihoods depended on it. If we could deliver pics that would make Gabriela—not to mention her "readers"—drool at the thought of being with us, or between us, then we could pretty much guarantee that Perry's phone would continue to "ring off the hook" in the new year.

"We're going to do some nudes, first," I said. "I have the angles and poses mostly worked out, but I need help with focus and metering. And lighting. It's a nice afternoon, so we can do a lot with natural light. But we'll have to fill, as well. It's a balancing act, Elly. If you meter for *me*, then Noah will look like a ghost. And if you meter for *Noah,* then I'll become a dark shadow.

"By that I mean, if you take an ambient reading of our bed with Noah in it, the white sheets will make him look tanned and lovely. Add me, and I'll become as interesting as a lump of coal. So we have to compensate with some fill light. Don't let Noah blow out, and don't let me disappear. Does that make sense?"

"Complete sense, Boss. Where do we start?" Elijah asked.

"We're going to strip. You strip, too," I said.

"You're joking," Elijah said.

"Do I look like I'm joking? Come on, Elly. Behave yourself. Get naked. We'll all be more comfortable. And besides, your skin color is close to mine. You can stand in while I set up lights." Noah and I dropped our robes—Elijah's robes—while Elly, reluctantly, pulled off his sweats and sneaks. And we went to work.

I started with Noah reclining on lots of plump pillows. I grabbed a few test shots I knew would be stunning. And then I said, "Elly, lie on top of Noah with your head on his chest." I thought Elijah's eyes would bug out of his head, like a cartoon character, but he did as he was instructed.

I had never really seen Elijah's body before. I knew it would be trim and cute, but I had made the mistake of thinking he was rather sexless. Instead, he's actually heartachingly masculine and totally desirable. When Elly slid into place—on top of my precious mate—I was unprepared for the rush of feelings that washed over me. Jealousy? Yes. Lust? Yes. Envy? Yes.

Noah automatically embraced Elijah—just as he would be holding me when we took the actual photos

Bruce K Beck

There were erections all around. I tried to arrange the lighting as quickly as possible. Noah was perfect in sunlight filtered through the studio skylights. His eyes shown translucent like violet tourmalines. I knew my own eyes were light-amber enough to also catch fire in that light. I didn't want to lose it.

I focused one lighting instrument, which was enough to warm Elijah/me sufficiently to create tonal balance. I said, "Okay, let's shoot this." Elijah scrambled out of Noah's embrace and took my place behind the camera. I took the position that Elijah had held so sweetly a few moments before. Noah welcomed me.

"Go for it, Elly," I said. "This is your shoot now. Photos by Elijah Montgomery. Has a nice sound to it. Don't you think?" Elijah dutifully framed and focused. And then he began to snap images of Noah and me. Noah was as comfortable in front of a camera as if it were just the two of us sharing an embrace. I tried to follow his lead.

Noah and I shifted our poses slightly. We kissed, we clung to each other, Elijah snapped. I sensed when he had caught the moment and when he had missed it. I knew there would be plenty of keepers. We changed the pose: I reclined on my side with Noah in front of me. I embraced him very much as I did when I spooned him at night. All night. Every night.

"Could you move my key light, Elly?" I asked. "See if you can light me more from above without spilling onto Noah. If it seems too complicated, I'll switch places and set the light for you. Take full frames, Elly. We can crop out genitals for 'family friendly' uses."

"I got it, Boss," he said. I doubt Elijah wanted to get back into bed with Noah without the chance of consummation, any more than I wanted to let go of the heavenly body in my arms. The camera shutter clicked, and I was satisfied that Elly was capturing the images we wanted.

After a few more poses, we put some clothes on and did the dewy-eyed shots for public consumption. Lots of smiles and teeth. They were so honest that they were nearly more fun to make than the nudes. "Are you satisfied?" I asked Noah.

"Yes, Toby."

"Elly?"

"Yes, Boss. Yo' two bes the prettiest couple I done ever seed. I's was feared the camera might most melt."

"Well since it didn't, I have an idea: Let's go skating before dinner," I suggested. "I'll call Perry and see if he can join us." And it was all arranged in a few moments. When Perry arrived, less than an hour later, I had already sent Elijah off to the skating rink to get us a place in line. Noah decided on a shower.

I welcomed Perry and poured him a glass of wine. "Where is everybody?" he asked.

"Noah's in the shower. Elijah is in the ticket line at the skating rink. I had a thought."

"Yes?"

"Perry, I think you should court Elijah. I don't want you to make the mistake that I made."

"And what might that be?"

"You know exactly what mistake I made, Perry. A decade ago. I ended our affair because I was too stupid to see how much I love you. With Elijah, you could have what we could have had if I had known how to grab it. He's a lot smarter than I was, our

Elly. He won't let you down the way I did, Perry.
Just saying!"

"You're a nice man, Toby."

"Anything I know about nice I learned from you,
Perry. Now, save your compliments for someone who
needs them. Get out of here!" Perry gave me a quick
kiss and then headed out to meet Elijah at the skating rink. Winter wonderland and all. Christmas in
New York. Great handfuls of fairy dust.

Noah emerged from the bathroom looking impos-
sibly beautiful. "Where's Perry?" he asked. "I
thought we were going skating."

"*They're* going skating. *We're* going back to bed,"
I said.

"Toby, you're a very nice man," Noah said.

"No," I said. "But I'm glad I have a few people
fooled."

The new year got off to a very cold start in New York City—the kind of temperatures we only experience once in a decade or so. With Charley still away in Singapore, a certain numbness had set in. I put on extra layers and went about my dreary work life, not knowing whether the cold in my heart was the result of climate or of loneliness.

But then just as the deep freeze eased a bit and we were experiencing the first real blizzard of the season, Charley announced that he was coming home! And suddenly a foot-and-a-half of snow felt as warm as a summer rain.

Charley asked me to share the news with Michael. They had been besties since their freshman year at Brown, after all. "Oh, Peter, that's wonderful news!" Michael said. "When does he get back?"

"The end of February, it looks like."

"Good," Michael said. "I'll arrange a little party for the first week in March—after you two have had some honeymoon time." I was grateful for Michael's generosity, of course, but all I really cared about was the prospect of having Charley back in my arms.

The weekly video calls had not been enough to keep me sane during our separation. And so maybe I took some chances while Charley was away. Maybe loneliness-induced madness encouraged me to explore some beds I'd have surely avoided if Charley had been beside me. But that was all in the past. Wasn't it?

The one good thing to come out of our separation was my discovery that Charley's best friend and *my* best friend were perfect for each other. I think my strong feelings for Rodney began when I dumped him and he forgave me. Maybe that's when I really learned to love him. If I had understood my feelings for Rodney when we were dating, perhaps everything would be different.

I won't call Rodney a size queen. Let's just say he knows his way around a big one. And Michael has the biggest one I've ever seen—or experienced. Had Michael not told me so himself, I wouldn't have believed that his endowment scared people and contributed to his being a single man who didn't want to be.

Rodney, of course, had no such fears. Once I realized that Rodney and Michael were meant for each other, I not only arranged for them to meet but then witnessed their nuptials a month later. So satisfying!

Other than that happy event, the months without Charley had been dreary indeed. And with the news of his homecoming, I began to worry about whether or not he still loved me. Perhaps I secretly worried about whether I still loved him! I needn't have.

I went to Charley's apartment to await his return. And the man who walked through his door and wrapped himself around me was the same hunk of perfection who had gone away on business in July. He even smelled the same! We picked up right where we had left off.

I would have preferred to keep Charley all to myself, but I knew I had to share him with Michael and our other friends. There was a dinner with Michael and Rodney shortly after Charley's return. And then, the following week, Michael's welcome-home gathering. He booked a party room at a midtown club. I knew it would be very elegant and very expensive. Charley was used to that. I was learning.

While Charley and I were dressing for Michael's party, Charley said to me, "Peter, I've never seen Michael so happy. I think it's brilliant—their marriage. I'm just sorry I couldn't have been there. It was your doing, Petey. Wasn't it?" I couldn't deny my matchmaking, but I didn't want to take too much credit.

Charley wrapped me in his arms and said, "I have a theory about their whirlwind romance—Michael and Rodney's. It would never have occurred to me to pair the two of them, and yet you knew, didn't you? You knew they were right for each other." I probably blushed a little.

"I want my friends to be happy," I said, "now more than ever. We've all been wandering around solo for too long: Rodney, Michael, you, and I. And now we're no longer alone!" It was a glorious feeling, actually—being partnered. That was no surprise, of course, but the reality of it was overwhelming.

"You boys look terrific," Michael said as he welcomed us to his club. The hospitality space was bigger than I expected. Those clubs look so quiet from the street. It's hard to know how spacious and accommodating they are until you experience them firsthand.

We thanked Michael, of course. Rodney greeted us and then returned to being nearly joined to Michael at the hip. I loved it—Rodney's happiness. And Michael's. And my own! If only I could give Charley that same feeling of joy. I was far from confident about my abilities.

It was a charming group of guests that Michael assembled: a few work friends of Rodney's and mine and associates of Charley's, including the tall, slim Japanese beauty I had admired so. I had never seemed to hear his name—which turned out to be Hiro. Dazzling smile. Great ass. Like that. And speaking of charming smiles and asses, Ajmal and his Uncle Salem were there.

Surely Charley knew that I bedded Ajmal while he was away. There was an inevitability about it from the moment we met at Michael's country house in Connecticut. In July. Perhaps if Charley had stayed in New York, I could have avoided Ajmal's mesmerizing smile. And touch. And kiss. And cock. But Charley answered the call to business in Singapore, so we'll never know.

I don't suppose my heart was ever in real danger—as my ass certainly was. An irresistible man plus an absent mate. These things can cloud one's judgment. And after all, hadn't Charley insisted I live my life while he was away? Hadn't he made it clear he was not expecting to come home to a saint? And bedding Ajmal was a one-time thing, after all.

If I'm going to be honest, I'll have to admit that I would have returned to Ajmal's bed—again and again—had he invited me. My Dubai beauty turned out to be the adult in the room: he knew perfectly well that I was meant for Charley, and he had no wish to fall into unrequited love. Smart, as well as hot as hell.

Uncle Salem was a slightly older version of Arab irresistibility. When I first met him—at Michael's in July—he flashed very much the same incandescent smile as his nephew. But while Salem never grabbed my ass or my cock (as Ajmal did) he was unmistakably all about sex. Sex and money, of course. At first I wanted to introduce him to Rodney. But I thought better of it. I didn't want to see my best friend wind up in a harem somewhere.

Jill and Sandi both came to the party. They were the friends who had accidentally introduced Charley and me the previous spring and then became part of our story. I didn't particularly know the other guests. Friends of Charley's and Michael's, mostly: Miffy and Buffy and Jocko and Whit. All of them perfectly pleasant and totally adoring of Charley.

The food, to my surprise, was quite wonderful. My favorite part was the ice mountain covered with oysters on the half shell. I always said that I never ate my fill of oysters. That night I did. The hot hors d'oeuvre were nicely seasoned and handsomely presented. And they were passed around by a very cute staff.

Michael was a remarkable host, as always. At one point he tapped his champagne glass and managed to achieve quiet long enough to propose a toast to Charley and me. I started to get teary when Michael referenced "my best friend," and "the perfect man to share his life." I hoped I really was that man. I prayed I was.

"Rodney and I are hoping the next time we all get together if will be for Charley and Peter's wedding,"

Michael said. A great cheer went up. Charley blushed slightly. I'm sure I did too. It was all kind of warm and wonderful, actually. And Charley seemed so happy! That was the best part.

I had relaxed into having a very good time at Michael's party when I saw Charley and Ajmal deep in conversation. It spooked me. It wasn't that Charley and I had secrets from each other, or even that I had committed some grave infidelity. I just felt that my attraction to Ajmal was somehow disloyal. Or something. And so I spent the rest of our charming evening with a sense of dread where before there had been mostly joy.

When we got home from the party that night, I asked Charley, "What did Ajmal say to you?" I'll admit I was a bit nervous. I had told Charley most of my history with Ajmal, but not the most romantic details. Most likely. Or perhaps I had mentioned things while assuming that Charley already knew. And then there were little white lies of omission. Or were they scarlet?

"He said he expected us to get married. He said that if I didn't marry you, I'd be a great fool, and that a fool and his treasure are soon parted. What do you think of that, Peter?"

"I think Ajmal is a wise man—as well as being a pistol-hot man." I figured I might as well admit my attraction. "Actually, I think you should marry me soon, Charley. I'm free on Thursday, around noontime. Does that work for you?"

"Do we have to wait that long? Couldn't it be Tuesday instead?" And then Charley kissed me. And then I knew precisely why I wanted to spend the rest of my life with him.

It wasn't quite that easy, of course. It never is. Within minutes of accepting the notion that Charley and I would wed, I asked, "Why me, Charlie? Why do you want to marry *me*?"

"Other than the fact that I'm desperately in love with you?"

Other than that," I said. "People fall in love with people every day. That doesn't make it a good idea or a good match."

"Peter, I thought you were more romantic than that," he said. "Did I fall in love with a cynic?"

"No, you fell in love with a fraidy cat," I said. "If you fell out of love with me, Charley, I'd most likely die," I said. "And I was hoping for a long life." It was the truth, really. I was terrified of the possibility of losing Charley and what we had found together.

"Since you asked," Charley said, "I can tell you that you give me everything I need, Peter. And you make me feel like ... like a complete person for the first time in my life. And you also make me feel like the sexiest man on Earth."

"That you are," I said. "Nothing to do with me. The first time we went home together, Charley, when I started to take off your clothes, I was afraid I might lose my nerve and head home. I had been to bed with dozens of hot guys. Okay, hundreds of hot guys. Probably. Who remembers? But I had never been with a man as exquisite as you are. And I wasn't sure I could satisfy you."

"Isn't that a little silly, Peter," he said, "coming from a man who has a perfect body?" That earned

Charley a deep kiss, of course. "What if I get down on one knee and propose to you?" Charley asked. "Would that help?"

"I doubt it," I said. "Besides, you always did your best work on *both* knees. Charley, I'm just afraid. I don't expect guarantees in life, but I also don't like to set myself up for heartache."

"Peter, my little Petey, my precious boy, my perfect mate, how can I reassure you? What will it take to calm your fears?"

"Well, a wedding band would help," I said.

"Done."

"And maybe if you told me precisely why you decided on *me*. That might help, too."

"That's easy," Charley said. "The night we met, when Jill and Sandi introduced us, I said to myself, 'Charley, he's the man for you. He's the *mate* for you. *He's* the one.'"

"Bullshit!" I said. "I don't believe you, Charley. I thought I was the only one who went there. You never told me exactly how you felt. You never told me that you...." I had love-at-first-sight right on the tip of my tongue, yet it seemed entirely too silly. And yet it was completely honest. "I took one look at you, Charley, and I said to myself, 'Self, he's your man. He's your future. He's the most wonderful creature on Earth. And you have to do whatever it takes to land him. You'll never find happiness any other way.'" It was all true, and of course admitting it made me feel even a bigger fool.

Charley went right into Charley mode. He swept me into his arms and kissed me sweetly. And then he said, "Well, now that we've established our origin story, I think we should get busy with wedding plans. Will you meet me at Cartier on Monday?"

"Of course, Charley," I said, "but marriage is a big fucking deal. Are you sure it's what you want? Just because Michael wants us to get married and Rodney wants us to get married and Ajmal wants us to get married, that's no reason for us to rush into something you might regret."

Charley waited patiently until I had finished sputtering. Then he said, "Is that it, Petey?"

"No," I said. "You don't even know me, Charley. How can you take a chance like this?"

"Well, you haven't told me yet if you had your teeth straightened when you were a teenager. But I'm sure you'll tell me when the time is right. That kind of getting-to-know-you? Is that what you mean?"

"No, Charley." I nearly told him about my Uncle Julius, but that story seemed too tame to make an impression. Instead, I went right for the deepest degradation: "I'm talking about how my cousin Steve used to take me to the basement in his parent's house and fuck the shit out of me. And how I let him do it. How I even liked it. And how I was damaged goods by age twelve. That's what I mean. And no, I never had my teeth straightened. Mom and Dad said they couldn't afford it."

Charley was quiet for a moment. Thoughtful. And then he said, "Peter, one of the things I love best about you is that you're a survivor. You have inner strength I could only just dream of possessing. I knew that—from the moment we met. So, if part of that power has to do with Cousin Steve, then so be it. I wish I could have been around when you were a child to protect you and to kiss away your hurts. But I wasn't. And since there was no one else to help you, you healed yourself. And that's why today you're the man I love with all my heart. I want to spend every moment with you, Peter, waking or sleeping. I think that could be the basis of a good marriage. What do you think?"

Well, of course I couldn't think of much of anything except that I had never been happier for a single moment in my whole miserable life. "And I like your teeth just the way they are," Charley said.

Well, we didn't do the deed that very week after all. It was too complicated. At first, we scheduled a service for noon on Thursday, so Rodney could be my matron of honor and then head back to our office to finish the day. And Ajmal agreed to stand up for Charley. And that gave us built-in witnesses. I considered, briefly, the potential for awkwardness, considering that I had shared memorable lovemaking with everyone in the wedding party.

But really, what's the point in dwelling on the past? Charley was the only man I wanted with my whole heart, and he was about to commit to our union not just emotionally but legally as well. Michael would have been Charley's best man, of course, except that he had to be in Bermuda for the annual gathering of the clan. All his wealth and good fortune came with some family obligations attached. He was resolved. Rodney was resolved, too.

Michael had urged him to make the trip to Bermuda. But Rodney refused either to miss my wedding or to be a source of disapproval for Michael's family at their annual disapproval convention.

Michael promised to throw a big party for us in the spring, and then he headed off where duty called.

I wasn't certain how Rodney would deal with the separation. He and Michael had spent every day together since their nuptials. It had been a lovely but low-key affair. And surely Rodney's memories of the day were much keener than mine. "Peter, this is torture," Rodney told me at lunch the day after Michael's departure. "And not in a good way."

"I know, Roddy," I said, "but you can handle it." The thought of being separated from Charley again sent shivers of pain up my spine. So, I got it. I truly understood Rodney's distress. "He'll be back in two weeks, Roddy," I said. "And Michael will want you more than ever." I was only stating the obvious, but it seemed like the sort of soothing talk that friends share. Rodney took a few deep breaths and then finished his lunch.

"Let's do this right," Charley said to me at dinner that evening. "We don't need to rush into anything. We could get married in the spring. It might be more fun if we plan it a little. The license is good for sixty days, and we already have the rings. And since they're being sized, there are no returns!"

Charley was right, of course. There was absolutely no reason for us to rush to City Hall that week. And yet, I had been so elated at the prospect of marrying Charley that the change in plans was deflating for me. Charley sensed my disappointment, of course, and he was particularly kind and gentle with me.

The rest of the week seemed gray, except that Charley held me in his arms every night as we went to sleep. Even when I sank into creepy visions of loss and danger and shouted myself awake, Charley was always right there, holding me. Keeping me safe. That created a level of perfection in my life that was far more powerful than wild dreams.

I was a bit surprised by Ajmal's call that Friday evening. He asked me to meet him for a coffee early the next week. I told Charley about the call, of course. And I wondered aloud about the point of our meeting. "Peter, don't you know you're irresistible?" Charley asked. "If I were Ajmal, I'd certainly want to see you."

"Ha, ha," I said. "Charley, I'm glad you're you and not Ajmal, but I'd be even gladder if you helped me out a little here." Charley kissed me. Deeply.

"Does that help?" he asked.

"It certainly does." And we left it at that.

"I think you both were very wise to delay your wedding ceremony until spring," Ajmal said over coffee that Tuesday afternoon. We met at a downtown spot with great coffee, excellent pastries, and other offerings, including maybe the best baguette in the city.

"In fact," Ajmal said, "I want you and Charley to be married at my place." *His place* is the top floor of a mid-town Manhattan high rise. The center space— very open and light-filled with southern and northern exposure—is his office, while Ajmal's apartment is the west end of the floor and his wife's apartment is the east end. I think I told you how I learned the geography.

"Ajmal, that is so generous of you," I said. "I don't know what to say."

"No, Peter. It's actually quite selfish of me. I want you and Charley to be married with all the comfort I can offer. Charley deserves it. He's a good man, and I've loved him for more than a decade. But you, Peter—you might have been my perfect mate had you not fallen in love with Charley first. I admitted defeat months ago, but I want one last chance to give you all the pleasure I can. You see, I want to stage the wedding and the reception in my office—the restaurant downstairs will arrange everything—and then I want you and Charley to honeymoon in my apartment."

"But, Ajmal," I sputtered, "where will *you* stay? We can't turn you out of your home."

He flashed his killer grin and said, "Peter, my wife and her school friend will be happily at home in Dubai with the children in May. She won't mind if I stay in her digs for a week or two."

"Ajmal, it seems too complicated," I protested.

"Peter, I had hoped you would understand the happiness it will bring me. The truth is, I want to know that the first time you and Charley make love as husbands, it will be in my bed. That makes me a part of your union. At least a bit. You won't deny me that satisfaction, will you, Peter?"

Once he put it that way, I didn't have the heart to protest further. But could I spend Charley's and my first night as legal mates in the splendid comfort of Ajmal's bedroom? The visions that danced in my head were of carpets and gilt furniture and over-stuffed luxury and—of course—intense physical passion shared with a beautiful man who was not the one who was about to become my husband.

I smiled and said, "I'll talk to Charley about it. Could I give you our answer tomorrow?" I felt some rumblings in my crotch as I headed back to the of-fice. I also felt some uneasiness about the whole situation.

I tried to sound casual at dinner that night when I told Charley about Ajmal's offer. Charley said, "That's so generous of him! But Peter, you don't seem very happy about the whole thing. Did you have something else in mind? We haven't really talked about our wedding day, have we?"

"No, I don't suppose we have," I said.

"Tell me everything you think and feel," Charley said. "Unless that's too tall an order." We smiled. I relaxed a bit.

"Charley, as long as we're together, I'm sure our wedding will be wonderful," I said. "I'll do anything you want. I'm cool with a church or a public space or the Observation Deck at the Empire State Build-ing."

"Hadn't thought of that," Charley said. "Now that would be romantic!"

"Indeed," I said. "And so would Ajmal's place. I've been there, you know." I figured I'd better get that out into the light.

"I assumed you had," Charley said, without any visible reaction. "Yes, it's a welcoming space. And Ajmal is a generous host. I'm sure our friends will be comfortable there. And his apartment would be an amazing place to honeymoon. Don't you think?"

"Yes. But is it the right place for *us*?" I suppose I could have said, *Are you sure you want to spend our wedding night in the bed where Ajmal fucked the shit out of me?* or, *Ajmal actually wants to be in bed with us. Are you okay with a threesome for our wedding night?* or, *What if we just book a hotel room in Ver-mont and honeymoon there?*

Instead, I said, "Charley, let's do whatever makes you happy. That's all that matters to me." It was the truth, of course. Charley embraced me.

"Petey, I don't think this is really so complicated," Charley said. "You're quite right. As long as we're together, it will be fine." I kissed Charley deeply, and he returned my passion. I wondered if I would ever get enough of him. I hoped not.

"Peter, I told you Hiro came to Singapore while I was there," Charley said, "in October, I think?"

"Yes."

"Well, I didn't tell you that he spent a night with me. He's a very attractive man, of course. He wanted to go to bed with me. We had never done that in New York. I was lonely. I agreed."

The thought of Charley making love to Hiro with his inky hair and radiant smile and creamy skin and perfect ass filled me with a swirl of emotions that quickly landed in my crotch—as most emotions do. The thought of Hiro—who is probably better hung than I am—in the embrace of the auburn perfection I had come to think of as my sole property sent my mind reeling.

"Why didn't you tell me at the time?" I asked.

"Because it seemed unnecessary and potentially hurtful."

"Why are you telling me now?"

"Because I think you have some similar experiences and feelings—with Ajmal—that are making you unhappy. I can't ask you to censor yourself, Peter. I can't ask you to ignore anything you remember or you feel. But I will ask you to share everything you can—including your life, if you're willing. I'll give you all of me. I want you, Peter."

"Warts and all?" I inquired.

"You don't have any warts, Petey," he said. "I've inspected your entire canvas, and I've yet to find a flaw. But if you develop some, they'll be grandfathered in."

"Let's leave my grandfather out of this. He was not a very nice man," I said.

"Well, his grandson is my idea of perfection," Charley said.

"Charley, will you really ...?"

"Yes."

"Can I really count on you ...?"

"Yes."

"Will you let me love you for the rest of my life?"

"Yes."

"Then why are we wasting time with trivial things?" I asked.

"Why, indeed?"

"Jess, I don't think you have enough warm clothes," I said to my beautiful young partner that February day when we were packing for our ski trip. His community college had a winter break, and we decided to accept an offer of hospitality at Larry and Peter's cabin in Maine.

"I don't know, David," Jesse replied. "I've never been to Maine in the winter. I've never been to Maine!" I embraced him, and then—because he's irresistible—I kissed him deeply. Jesse kissed me back. Surely that was it. Surely my obsession with him had much to do with the fact that Jesse always seemed to want exactly what I wanted. What I needed. From him.

"We should go to Paragon this afternoon and get some of those thermal sweats or something," I said. "I don't know. We'll figure it out. I don't want you to freeze your ass off. It's a beautiful ass. And I'd never forgive myself if something bad happened to it."

That time it was Jesse who came to me with a kiss. And a proposal: "David, do you think we have time, before we go shopping, for you to demonstrate how much you like my ass?"

"There's always time for that," I said. I took his hand and we headed to bed. We tumbled and bounced and giggled like teenagers. Actually, Jesse *was* a teenager. But I felt like one, too, when I was with him. I was glad that he had turned nineteen the previous month. It made me feel slightly less pervy than I had felt when I fell in love with an eighteen-year-old the summer before.

I was hardly a dirty old man—at thirty-five—but even so, I had been uneasy about our age difference. No, not the difference in our ages but Jesse's extreme youth. I wondered if it was healthy for him—at such a tender age—to make a commitment to me. I wondered if I could give him everything he deserved.

Most of all, I think I wondered if I had any right to expect Jesse to choose to be mine, when he had relatively little experience of men. I should say, Jesse had few *healthy* experiences of men. Plenty of the other kind. Like most of us. Harvey, my best friend, told me not to worry. He said Jesse chose me because I'm perfect for him. And perfectly loveable. I wasn't so certain.

What if Jesse met some nice guy more his own age and decided to explore the possibilities? Would I encourage him? Would I then welcome him home after the exploration had run its course? What if Jesse got invited to an orgy? Would I urge him to go? And what if I were also invited? Would I join him? Would I be able to watch others enjoying Jesse's perfect young body and then go home with him as if nothing of importance beyond physical pleasure had happened?

I wanted Jesse to have all the experiences a young man should have. I won't list the possibilities. But how could I ask Jesse—or allow him—to miss out on even just my own catalogue of sexcapades, for instance, many of which were memorably delightful.

No, Jesse deserved to have every possible experience—within reason, of course. He deserved every possible pleasure.

So how could I be certain that Jesse got every experience he needed while at the same time he remained mine alone? Hmmm. Tricky. I put those thoughts on hold, more or less, while I got on with our Saturday. "Let's head over to Union Square," I suggested. "After we shop, we can get a bite to eat nearby."

Shopping and preparing for a new adventure are always exciting. Everything that Jesse and I did together was exciting that year. Everything seemed new and festive. Even shopping for warm outerwear at Paragon. "Jess, try this on." I said.

"Davey, I have a down jacket. It's plenty warm."

"But try this," I insisted. "It's engineered for light-weight warmth on the ski slopes, I think. Anyway, even if you get caught in an avalanche, this will keep you safe." I only wished I could really find ways to keep Jesse safe. Perhaps I wondered why we have so few tools for safety in this life—for ourselves, let alone for the few others we'd gladly open a vein for.

Jesse agreed. He slipped into the parka thing with the hood and all the special Velcro closures around the openings. It was feather-light and yet stubbornly rugged at the same time—like armor that has morphed into a new kind of skin. And the mossy color made his eyes sparkle like freshly polished sapphires. "Okay, that's decided," I said.

"Do I have a say in this?"

"No, not in this," I said. "You get to decide what we have for dinner." Jesse flashed me his quizzical look, as if he wondered how far he might get if he resisted my decision. "You need new gloves," I said.

Jesse followed me obediently to the glove department. We quickly found a warm pair that looked great with the new parka. Done. And off to a falafel dinner.

"I haven't seen Jayden in ages," I said to Harvey at lunch on Monday. "Not since Jesse started at LaGuardia in January and cut back his hours at the kennel. How is Jayden, anyway?"

"He's ... fine," Harvey said. "I wish he had a little more ... direction. I want him to get an education, but he seems content to work with dogs all day. For now, anyway. I'm not complaining, David. Jayden has dinner with me every night, and he warms my heart and my bed. I couldn't love him more if I tried. I don't have to tell you how precious he is."

"No, Harv. I get it, believe me." Jayden was indeed precious—nearly as precious as Jesse! And it was uncanny how much the two of them looked alike. Had Jayden not acquired some African DNA from his family tree, they might have been mistaken for twins.

"I'm glad Jesse decided to start school in January," Harvey said. "I'm sure he'll make a fine veterinarian—if that's what he wants."

"And Jayden will figure out what he wants, too," I said. "Who knows? Maybe they'll set up a practice together. I can see it: the two handsomest vets in New York City caring for all your pets' needs. Sounds like a winner!"

"And Jayden could head the boarding and grooming part of the practice, if he decides against getting a degree," Harvey said. "Not only is he smart, but he's so intuitive about dogs. And they take to him. He meets a new dog and, within seconds, he has a new best friend. It's uncanny."

"You're right, Harv," I said. "I've seen it! Jesse, too, you know. Maybe I should grow a bushy tail and learn to bark."

"I think Jesse loves your tail just the way it is, Davey. I know I do."

"Thanks, Sweetie," I said. "And I love your tail, too. Now, what do you think about skiing? Should I give it a try?"

"Don't be stupid, Davey! You were always the perfect après-ski bunny—speaking of cute tails. Stick with that!"

"I think you're right," I said. "I just want Jesse to have everything. This ski holiday is perfect for him. Something new. And he'll get to spend a lot of time with Peter. Who's closer to his age. And drop-dead gorgeous. Just saying. Why am I nervous?"

"Shut up, David!" Harvey said. "You and Jesse are going to have a lovely winter holiday. And when you come home from Maine, you two will be closer than ever."

"Yes, dear," I said. Did I believe it? Maybe. Partially, at least. "But what if Jesse decides that Peter is his ideal man? Or Larry? Larry is also extremely attractive. Old enough to be Jesse's father, of course, but most men are. Harvey, I don't think I can handle this trip."

"Hush, little Davey," Harvey said. "You can handle anything. And you know it." Harvey had a point, of course. I had been coping with all the nonsense life threw my way for thirty-five years, after all. And I had no real reason to expect imminent danger. Yet

Bruce K Beck

I was uneasy as Jesse and I finished packing for our trip.

I had visions of a romantic winter train ride to New England with my beloved, but that turned out to be more time-consuming than we could manage in a long weekend. Larry said, "Just fly to Portland, and there's a bus to Bridgton that's easy to access from the airport. We'll meet you in town." And it was decided.

Jesse seemed so casual about our trip. I was developing my usual travel nerves as we packed and checked my list and double-checked all the details. Eventually, of course, we got ourselves out of the apartment and into a waiting Uber bound for LaGuardia airport. Jesse mostly smiled. But then that's his nature.

I've never quite understood how Jesse turns turbulence into calm. A rare gift, that. It's not that I'm a drama queen, exactly. Most of the time—especially at work—I'm sensible and solid. But I'll confess to occasional flights of fantasy and near-panic that are not particularly well grounded in reality.

Harvey was the first man who understood me— when we were in our mid-twenties. He always knew what to say and what to do to bring me back to Earth after a mini episode of panic. Had I been smarter about the whole thing, Harvey and I might still be together. But there's no point in going there! Everything unfolded as it should have. As it always does.

"Welcome to Maine," Larry said as he greeted us at the bus stop in the middle of Bridgton. It was a beautiful day—cold and clear as a bell. Peter stowed our stuff in the rear of the SUV, and Jesse and I piled into the back seat. The trip up the mountain from town was only about fifteen minutes. Jesse smiled the whole way, as usual. I tried to relax.

When we arrived, Peter and Jesse went to greet the dog and to put away some groceries the guys had bought at the store in town. As we were heading into the cabin, Larry said, "My favorite aunt and uncle bought this place in the sixties. They didn't have any children, so they wanted me to have it. And when they met Peter, they decided the time had come to pass the torch. Aunt Elly and Uncle Steve live in a sort of retirement community near Portland that will become assisted living for them when they need it. When we first took over the cabin, they used to come here for a few weeks in the summer and a week or so during ski season. But it's really all ours now."

"It's so comfortable and inviting, Larry," I said. Larry acknowledged my compliment with a smile, but he seemed less than convinced.

"I don't know, David. I love this house, but it's so far from New York. If Peter didn't look forward to coming here, and if I didn't love my aunt and uncle so much, I'd be tempted to sell it and move on. But that's a decision for another day. Let me show you your room. The bed came with the house. The mattress is stuffed with horsehair, according to legend. Elly and Steve always thought of it as their marriage bed, and it really is amazingly comfortable. It's only just a double, but I think you two will be comfortable there."

"I'm sure we will," I told Larry. I also embraced him and got a little weepy.

"David, are you okay?" Larry asked me.

"I'm fine," I answered. "Just a little tired. I'm not a natural traveler." That was the truth, of course. But the whole truth? Maybe not so much.

"Why don't you and Jesse settle into your room?" Larry said. "There's no schedule here. Take a nap, if you like." I thanked him, and Jess and I did indeed heft our bags to our new room. We didn't really unpack, but we did test the famous bed, which was even more comfortable than legend had claimed. Jesse beside me; Jesse in my arms again. It was just what I needed.

We surfaced after our little nap, and Larry said, "Let's drive over to the lodge. I should have told you. They just renamed it: it's no longer Shawnee Peak. They decided to restore the original name, which is Pleasant Mountain. I thought that was a little silly, but it's still a beautiful place."

The four of us gathered our things—ski paraphernalia for the ski boys and thick cashmere sweaters for Larry and me—and we piled back into the SUV for the short drive to the lodge. When we arrived, the boys headed for the ski lift area to rent skis and get themselves ready for an afternoon on the slopes. Peter said to me, "Don't worry, David. Jesse will be safe with me." He embraced me, and then Peter kissed me—rather sweetly—which was welcome but not especially reassuring as to Jesse's safety.

"Thanks, Peter," I said, not knowing how I really felt about the entire situation. Larry took me under his wing, leading me to the lodge with its vaulted ceilings and expanses of weathered timbers and sparkling views.

"Let's have a glass of wine," Larry suggested. I needed no coaxing. The bar was a bit off to one side and away from the relentless cheerfulness of all the sunlight in the main rooms. Perhaps bars should always have low lighting. They generally do, after all. We perched on barstools that were remarkably comfortable. "Chardonnay?"

"Sure," I said.

"Peter is very accomplished at this, David. I don't want you to worry about Jesse. Peter will make certain he proceeds at his own pace. Safely." I went for a smile and a thank-you, and I succeeded, pretty much.

Larry said, "I brought a couple of books along. I just finished reading Bruce K Beck's SUCH A GOOD MAN. I think it's his latest novel—and certainly his best. I loved it. You're welcome to give it a try. We don't have any plans until dinner, so if you just want to sleep in front of the fire, that's fine, too."

"Thanks, Larry," I said. "For everything. I was wondering—is there a deck somewhere for watching the skiers? Should we give them our moral support?"

"Yes, but there's not really much to see. They'll be out of sight in seconds. We can go out if you want. It's a beautiful day, and we're dressed warmly enough." And so Larry and I headed to the observation deck so that I could try to show loyalty—and perhaps a bit of mother hen—to my precious young mate.

We saw Jesse and Peter on the lift, so we knew they had already made one downward foray without mishap. They saw us, too, and waved. So, that was our display of solidarity. Skiing seems to be only a spectator sport at the Olympics. Larry and I went back inside.

The lodge was furnished to give it a rustic look—befitting the setting—while at the same time it was amazingly comfortable. So, did I fall asleep in front of the fire? Yes, for maybe an hour. And then I picked up the novel Larry brought along for me. No more napping after that!

By 5:00, things on the slopes were winding down. I had nearly forgotten how short northern winter days are. I should have remembered the February I had spent in Boston once. It's also in the Northeast, but so much grayer, earlier, than New York City. And there we were at an even higher latitude. I was ready for the day to melt into sunset.

"I'm sure the boys will change and meet us here in a few minutes," Larry said. "Peter knows what time our dinner reservation is."

"I could go and check on them," I said. Whatever that meant.

"Sure, David. We rented Changing Room #7 for the weekend. But no doubt they'll be here shortly." I wanted to relax and wait calmly with Larry for our mates and dinner companions to join us. I wanted to. But I couldn't do it.

"So, the 'Club House' is that way?" I inquired. And then I headed off to find Changing Room #7. I'm normally very polite and respectful of others' privacy. Normally. That February evening, I gave a quick tap on the door and barged right in. My behavior was rewarded accordingly.

Jesse and Peter had obviously just gotten out of the shower, and they were sharing a kiss. A friendly kiss, no doubt. But there were also semi-erections involved. Jesse sprinted over and embraced me while Peter went about the business of getting dressed. "So, what do you think of skiing?" I asked Jesse as cheerfully as I could manage.

"It was great. You should come with us tomorrow," Jesse said.

"Maybe I will," I said, trying not to shoot Peter a sidelong glance. Everything I most wanted for Jesse and everything I most feared for myself came together in that moment. Really, why shouldn't Jesse have the chance to kiss a very handsome, very nice young man? Why not, indeed? I'm embarrassed to admit it, but the two of them looked so beautiful together when I burst in on them that I began to feel rumblings in my crotch that seemed entirely inappropriate. And yet they were entirely real.

"I think we're still in good time for our dinner reservation," I said, lamely. "I'll just go back to the lodge and tell Larry we can expect you two in—ten minutes?"

"Perfect," Peter said. I felt like an idiot as I found my way slowly back to the fireplace in front of which Larry was still ensconced in warmth and comfort.

"Yes, of course, the boys will be along shortly," I said as casually as I could manage.

"I think you'll like the food here," Larry said. "It's a little heavy, but it is winter, after all. You can't go wrong with a steak and creamed spinach. I love the lamb chops. Peter loves the lobster thing. They really do get lobsters trucked in every day from a lobster pound in Portland." I smiled as naturally as I could manage.

Dinner was delightful. Or rather, I can say that the lodge offered terrific hospitality. I was pleased that Larry ordered a bottle of inexpensive—for a restaurant—Italian red (not that any restaurant bottle is reasonable these days, but let's not go there). It softened the prickly feelings at the edges of my brain.

And the second bottle washed down the very good food with remarkable smoothness.

It was very *Moonlight in Vermont* as Larry drove us expertly back to the cabin. Except, of course, we were two states over. So much for accuracy in nostalgia. I wondered if Jesse had ever heard of Margaret Whiting, let alone her hit songs. I wondered if he needed to carry around that kind of cultural baggage. It had seemed natural to me as a young gay boy to absorb the past like a sponge. Maybe Jesse would be different. Maybe he would prefer to travel light. As long as he wanted to travel with me, it didn't seem to matter.

"We usually turn in early here," Larry said as he put a sliver of a log on the fire, and we relaxed into that quiet time before bed. Brandies were poured. Just a tiny one for Jesse. He looked so pretty in the firelight that I feared I might lose any remaining sense of composure. A few sniffles and minor cough-like eruptions, and I was nearly myself again.

Jesse put his head on my chest as he settled into the comfort of our embrace and the Adirondack loveseat (or whatever they call mountain cabin style in Maine). The dog, Chester, wandered over to explore his guests. He was dutifully rewarded with lots of affectionate petting.

Chester had fallen instantly in love with Jesse, of course. He appeared to like me, too, which was gratifying. Dogs always seem to me to be excellent judges of character. So if one takes to me, then can I assume I might be all right after all? Hard to say.

When the brandies were finished, Peter and Jesse went to put the house—and Chester—to bed for the night. Larry said to me, "David, you know Peter was really just a boy when we met. Actually, I think Jesse is more mature than Peter was at his age. I think you know that it's a little scary to navigate at times. But always worth it."

"I just want him to be happy," I said as quietly as I could manage. Larry grabbed me and held me close.

Larry said, "I'm only going to say this once, David. And then we never need to go there again: You saved Jesse's life. You took him in and loved him when he had no other viable options. He knows it. And he worships you for it. And wherever the future leads, you two have that bond. It's unbreakable."

I thanked Larry for being a wise friend, and then I headed to our room. I was a little nervous about being alone with Jesse for the first time since my poor behavior at the ski lodge. I needn't have been, of course. When Jesse joined me in that comfy bedroom and began to strip for sleep, he still seemed to reflect the sparkle of the firelight. And I realized that I adored him with every fiber of my being.

When Jesse slipped into bed beside me, I savored him in my arms. I wondered if he smelled a little like a freshly shampooed puppy or maybe my only real friend in grammar school, whose underwear I had twice purloined—for sniffing purposes, of course. Actually, Jesse smelled of himself alone—a scent that permeated my head with the delicacy of a wildflower and the urgency of a rare essential oil.

We could have drifted off to sleep together. I could have been silent. That was my intention. But

I couldn't seem to manage it. "Did you like Peter's kiss?" I asked.

"Of course, David. He's a good kisser. So?"

"His dick is bigger than mine," I said. Yes, I descended there—into the depths of pissing contests and crossed swords and territoriality. I wasn't proud of it. But I wasn't able to stop myself, either.

"Actually, you're wrong, David. Your dick is bigger than his." It was a simple statement of fact—or perception. And the Size Police were nowhere around to offer their expert judgment. Jesse didn't follow his statement with *Does that make you happy?* or *Am I supposed to care about that?* or even *So what?*

And then I began to weep softly. Jesse turned and held me and waited patiently while I emptied the well—the *cistern* of negativity that had gurgled up into my consciousness.

"Are you angry with me?" Jesse asked.

"No," I answered, truthfully. "Just scared. I couldn't bear to lose you, Jess. Not to be dramatic, but I think it would kill me." That was a very adult shitload of guilt to dump on a very young man with issues of his own. But he shouldered it instantly.

"David, I would never do anything to hurt you," Jesse said.

"No, I don't believe you would. Not intentionally."

"What if I promise never to be alone with Peter again. Would that make it better?"

"I don't want promises, Jess," I said. "I just want your love. It really is that simple."

"Fuck!" Jesse said. "Is that what we're talking about?" And then he began to laugh. It took me a few seconds to grasp the absurdity of the situation. But I got it. And then my laughter matched Jesse's.

And then the two of us slowly wound down to chuckles, and then to quiet. A few very sweet kisses, and we could assume our favorite sleep positions and settle into a very comfortable bed, in preparation for a long winter's nap.

I wanted everything to be perfect for Sean's homecoming. It wasn't the day after Thanksgiving, as I had hoped. It wasn't even the day after Christmas. It was closer to New Year's Eve. Appropriate, anyway. Sean and I would be creating a new life together, after all. And what could be more auspicious than combining a new life and a new year?

When I greeted him at my apartment door, Sean seemed both the same and transformed. Was there a new radiance about him? Or a new confidence? He was the same beautiful boy I had fallen for the previous summer, but his stay with his family in Chicagoland that autumn had given him time to grow. Or something. Of course, I immediately began to worry whether he had _outgrown me_ while he was away.

Sean's kiss told me that we were still one. I attempted to relax a little. "Alex, you'll never know how much I missed you," Sean said.

"I'll bet I can guess," I replied. We kissed some more. And this was all before Sean took off his new leather jacket with the plush lining! And then we went about the business of getting Sean settled in. Even though he had lived with me for several months in late summer and early fall, perhaps it had been more of a sleepover, really, than a cohabitation. This time the arrangement felt different. More adult, maybe?

Perhaps I shouldn't have been so shocked when Sean vanished in November. Perhaps he had never been the partner I had imagined. Perhaps he had just been a live-in lover whom I mistook for my soulmate. Perhaps I have a tendency to overanalyze things.

"Rory says 'welcome home,'" I said.

"He's been a good friend to both of us, hasn't he?" Sean said. "As well as being one of the hottest men on the planet."

"Correct on both scores," I replied. I said a little silent prayer of gratitude for having Rory in my life. I don't really pray, but I did, that December afternoon, as I thanked the Universe for Rory's friendship. So many joys and pleasures through the years. So much glorious, uncomplicated sex. And— as I had only discovered in recent years—such unconditional love.

"Rory wants us to have dinner with him next week," I told Sean. "I said I'd ask you."

"Of course," Sean said. "I wonder if I've ever thanked him properly for introducing us. Probably not."

"Sean, you look terrific," I said.

"Thanks, Alex," he said. "You, by the way, look like a wet dream come true." That earned him a deep kiss.

"You don't have to dream, Sean. I'm right here. For as long as you want me." It was that kind of homecoming. I helped Sean unpack his things and arrange them on his side of the chest of drawers and on his side of the closet. The silk robe in rainbow hues that I had given Sean earned pride of place in the middle of the closet. I had never been able to rock it. It obviously belonged to Sean now.

I was bursting with questions for him. I forced myself to be nearly silent. I smiled a lot. I kissed him often. He seemed nearly as happy to be home as I was to have him. Nearly. When we had stowed Sean's things, he began to undress.

"Where's your buddy Dickie," I asked, referring to Sean's silicon "prosthesis" he had stuffed his briefs with, in the months he lived with me.

"He got lost along the way," Sean said. "I think we outgrew each other."

"It happens," I said. I was glad that Sean no longer needed to present a big-basket picture to the world. I fell in love with him just the way he is, and I had hoped he would learn to accept himself—and me—as is. I was also pleased to see that Sean had stopped shaving his chest. Where his naked skin had glowed like a baby's butt, there was now a soft sprinkling of gingery fur that added a new dimension to his slender torso. Macho? No, not Sean. Masculine? Surely.

When Sean held me against his chest he seemed to send new sexual sparks throughout my body. Or was that largely imaginary? Anyway, the new fur accentuated the baldness of his ample nipples, making them easier targets for oral attacks. I would surely take advantage of their new vulnerability.

"Sean, please, will you let me make love to you?"
"It's been a long day, Alex. I'm sticky."
"Good," I said.
"Let me just brush my teeth," he said.
"If you insist."

When Sean returned from the bathroom, I welcomed him into my bed—*our* bed. "Come, Baby. Let me warm you up," I said. He dropped his robe and slipped between the sheets. And then, finally, I had Sean's naked body in my arms again. Everything I remembered about the feel of his skin and the warmth of his kiss and the beauty of his limbs came true again.

"I didn't know, Sean," I said. "I didn't know if you were coming back to me."

"Hush, Alex," he said. "I'm here." Indeed. I put aside my fears, for the most part, and relished the beauty in my arms. I wanted Sean to know just how much I adored him, so I began a careful, rather quiet worship of his perfect body, from the freckle on his right eyelid all the way to his tasty toes—with lots of stops in between. As before, the central terrain proved to be my favorite. Sean's neat little navel might have been unremarkable had it not anchored the gingery stairway that led me to the exquisite sweetness between Sean's legs.

I never thought too very much about how Sean is made. When Rory told me he was different from the two of us, I wondered, of course, if I would mind. I wondered how I would feel the first time we made love. I wondered how I would like having sex with a man who lacked a pair of balls. I like balls. I *love* balls. But the instant I encountered Sean's body, I thought, *Oh. He has a different way of being a man. Who'd have thought that was possible?*

Was Sean's body really that unremarkable to me? Maybe. But most of all, I was so drawn to him that nothing else seemed to matter. A handsome face? Yes. Shoulders and arms that could stop traffic? Yes. A chest that was all about masculine strength?

Yes. Perfect ass? Yes. So, big balls? No. So, big dick? No. So what?

Sean let me savor his sweetness for rather a long time before he took my face in his strong hands and encouraged me to slide forward until our lips met. His trim beard and moustache tickled my nose. And then he said, "Please, Alex, I need you inside me." Had I required encouragement—or direction—that would have done it. Sean welcomed me into the warmth of his interior.

Mostly, I wanted to be the best lover I could manage to be. Considerate, thoughtful, attentive, and rock-hard. Surely Sean knew how much I wanted to please him. And he seemed to want me as much as I wanted him. When he threw his legs around my waist, we became one creature, joined in love. Or so I hoped.

I would have stayed in that embrace for eternity, had it been possible. But nothing that good can last forever. My epicenter—in my pelvis, of course—began to rumble with the need to explode. And when Sean's movements left me almost bouncing on top of him, I knew I couldn't delay the eruption much longer. And when Sean began to shout, I became hopelessly molten.

We seemed to flow into each other as if our borders had shifted. I no longer felt like just Alex. Sean had become a part of me, as surely as if our bodies had fused with the heat of our union. And even when I no longer had the bedrock for proper penetration, I remained inside of Sean. And when it seemed maybe like the time for me to pull out and flop back onto my bed, I wasn't certain Sean would release me. I wasn't certain he could.

Sean was also in no hurry for us to uncouple. Or so it seemed. I'm not stupid. I know where I've been and what I've done. But I often seem to need a little confirmation. I didn't have to wait long. "Alex, that was like nothing I've ever experienced," Sean said. "I don't have words for it."

"We don't need words, Baby," I said. And I meant it. But I did need words to order in a pizza for our supper. When we had reluctantly separated our bodies and pulled on some jeans and hoodies, it was time to make a little sense of real life. We set the table, and I opened a bottle of red.

The delivery was prompt. We smiled a lot, and we held hands a lot, between bites. I had promised myself I would not bring up the past. Not that homecoming evening. Not so soon after Sean's return. Ah, broken promises!

"Sean, why did you leave me?" I asked.

His reply was prompt but thoughtful—suggesting that his actions had been carefully considered and reconsidered. "Because I had to deal with some old business. Because I had to be sure I was worthy of your love."

"And why did you come back?"

"Because I couldn't imagine living without you."

That earned Sean a big sloppy kiss flavored with pizza sauce. But I couldn't leave it at that, of course. "I probably hoped you'd say you didn't want to break my heart."

"I didn't," Sean said. "And I don't want to break mine, either."

It sounded reasonable. I decided to retire that line of questioning for the night—a decision I sensed I could honor. We straightened up the dining table and the kitchen, and then we retired to the bedroom for cuddles and a new Netflix series. As Sean lay in my arms, the smell of his hair filled my senses, leaving me intoxicated. Sean's scent put red wine to shame. "Mere alcohol doesn't thrill me at all," etc.

I was just sober enough to rejoice in the fact that it was a Friday night, so my drug-of-choice and I could look forward to the entire weekend together before the reality of Monday morning settled in on us. Surely all of that could wait while Sean and I celebrated his return—quietly and privately.

It was just shy of midnight when I squeezed my new pet—my Irish-Setter-only-better—and said, "Come to sleep, Baby." He responded to my caress with a simple need to be close to me. Or so I hoped. We slept in each other's arms.

❦

"I just got a text from Mike," Sean said as I was making coffee in the morning. Mike was his best friend from the bakery café where Sean had worked. "He's in Seventh Heaven since Rory texted him. They're getting together on Saturday." Rory had, after all, promised Mike a date just as soon as Sean came safely home to me.

"Ah, yes," I said. "Mike's a cute little thing. I hope he's ready for The Full Rory!" We both laughed, knowing full well what it's like to receive Rory's full attention.

"How do you suppose he does that?" Sean asked.

"I don't know," I said, "but if we could bottle it, we could make a fortune." I thought a little more about our hot friend, and I said, "You know, it's not that it's effortless for Rory. He works very hard at bringing pleasure to other men. So hard that they naturally see to it that he gets his. Rory always gets his. But he earns it! For the moments you're in Rory's arms, you're the most precious creature on Earth. And if he happens to grace you with his orgasm, then you are twice blessed. Or thrice blessed. Or...?

"It's only slightly different when *you* hold me, Alex."

"How so?"

"I feel all of that from *you*, Alex," Sean said, "only your embrace tells me you want me forever. Rory's not a forever-type guy." That seemed true enough, and yet I wondered if the right man could domesticate our Rory. Or captivate his heart to the point where he would yearn to "forsake all others."

I had seen Rory and tasted him and felt him and watched him through the years as he showed me the most exquisite tenderness. He had moved me to tears on several occasions, and yet he had never slept in my bed. Except for that recent, very black period in my life when Sean was absent. Rory made himself entirely present when I needed him most.

"Let's plan to meet both of them for dinner some time the following week, then," I said. "I predict Mike will be wearing a very silly grin all evening."

"I'm certain of it," Sean said. "Like mine!" Was I even capable of bringing that sort of joy to another human? I doubted it. Sean seemed to think it was possible. I was willing to give it a try. Perhaps Rory and I were not all that different after all. Perhaps my need to please Sean would make me the lover he deserved. Perhaps I needed to quiet my brain and get on with life.

"Are you starting school soon?" I asked. That was a topic I had planned to avoid. Best laid plans.

"I think so," Sean said.

That was not the reply I had hoped to hear. "What does that mean?" I asked a little coldly, probably.

"I have an appointment in the bursar's office a week from Wednesday. They say there's a question of whether they received payment in time to admit me for this semester. I think I can fix it."

"Good," I said. Did I really care if Sean restarted his college studies immediately? What if he took the term off and simply devoted his attention to being mine? Wouldn't that be logical in some ways? I had a good job—if not a great job—so I could support Sean, couldn't I? If it came to that?

I tried to resist the urge to weigh in on the topic. Surely it was none of my business. Surely Sean could sort out his education and employment needs without interference from me. "Whatever happens at the bursar's office," I added, "we'll be fine, Darling. I don't want you to feel pressured. I have no expectations." It was largely true.

"What should we do today?" Sean asked.

"On your first day home? I think we should spend the morning in bed and then go out for lunch. And there's a show at the Met Museum I've been wanting to see. It's about ancient architecture. I think you'll find it interesting, too."

"Perfect," Sean said. "Bed first." And that's what we did.

"You two look ... radiant!" Rory said at our dinner date. It was good to be with my best friend. I hadn't seen him for a while, and I had missed him terribly without really knowing it. More than a week of Sean in my arms and Sean in my bed had preoccupied me, of course. I had spoken with Rory on the phone a few times. But it wasn't the same as actually being with him.

"Mike, is Rory being nice to you?" I asked flippantly. Everyone laughed. Mike was wearing the silly grin I had predicted, and he blushed beet red. That answered my question. "Just as I suspected," I said. That earned me more laughter.

"You leave Mikey alone," Rory said as he grabbed Mike and kissed the top of his head. "He's a good sport." Indeed. He was also exceptionally cute in a boyish way. I wondered if Rory could actually fall for him. I wondered how I would feel if Rory were suddenly partnered, after all these years. Not that Rory's choices had anything to do with me.

It was a good reunion for me and for Sean, I think. He and Mike hadn't seen each other since October. They had a natural bond based on age and gender identity, I guess. When Sean said, "Alex, I'm going to head back to Mike's place to pick up the last of my things," it seemed perfectly reasonable. And yet, the moment the two of them left the restaurant and disappeared into the night, I became anxious.

Rory was still there, of course. And he was looking at me in a slightly quizzical way. He took my hand and said, "I'm ordering drinks for us." Which he did. And then he said, "Alex, I've missed you. But I don't have to tell you that. You know how I feel about you."

I looked into his beautiful, dark eyes and said, "I think I do, actually. I think it's similar to how I adore you." That earned me a warm smile.

"How's my buddy?" he asked.

"Rory, you know how to ask the tough questions." I considered my reply while the server brought us scotch and cleared the last of the dinner things. There was also a complimentary sweet—a sort of shortbread finger with a piping of Nutella on it. Unbidden but entirely welcome. I asked for a coffee. Rory decided on an espresso.

When I had used up my fair allotment of time for stalling, I said, "Maybe I never thought too much about the future, but everything has changed, Rory. Now that Sean is back with me, I want everything to be perfect. And I want it to last. He's in my blood, Rory. I don't think I could live without him."

"Hush, Alex," Rory said. "We're not going there. Not tonight, anyway. And not anytime soon. Look, when I met Sean last summer he was a cute little boy who was desperate to make a connection. And now he's a handsome—and very smart—young man who has found purpose in his life. How do you suppose that happened?"

"You tell me," I said.

"It's you, Alex. But I don't have to tell you that. You know what your love is capable of." I wasn't so sure. I had loved Ben, surely, and yet he had left me for another man. I loved Rory, and yet he had never even considered being my mate. Probably. And now Sean. How could I entertain rosy thoughts for the future?

"Thanks, Rory," I said. "I wish I shared your optimism."

"It's not about optimism, Alex," he said. "Let's face some facts here: You happen to be one of the most desirable men on Earth ..."

"Likely!"

"Don't interrupt. Sean found you. He wants you. And he's not going anywhere. It's quite simple, really. Now, let's enjoy our beverages." And that's what we did. I hated saying good night to Rory, even though it meant I would soon have Sean in my arms. Why does life have to be so complicated?

It was the following Wednesday when I got a bit of a shock at the office. A building project I had been working on—a large complex in Houston with luxury housing and affordable housing and two theaters and public spaces—suddenly fell into my lap. I was expected to be in Houston to represent my firm during the final design decisions. February and March, probably. And maybe April as well.

I don't often travel for business, so it was surprising. But most of all, of course, I didn't know how I would tell Sean. How would he feel about leaving New York so soon after settling in? He would come with me, surely. Wouldn't he? We had never discussed travel or relocating or anything like that. We had never discussed lots of things.

When I got home from work on Wednesday, Sean greeted me with a radiant smile and a big kiss. "I have some wonderful news, Alex," he told me excitedly. "I'm going to pour you a glass of wine."

"I have some news as well," I said apprehensively, "but you can go first." We settled in on the sofa with glasses of my favorite bargain chardonnay. "What's going on?" I asked.

"I had a good meeting at the bursar's office today," Sean said, "and I start classes at Lehman College next week!" Sean fell into my arms, and I tried my best to congratulate him. "They accepted my credits for transfer, and I can start a degree program in the School of Social Work immediately!"

"Sean, that's fabulous!" I said. "I'm so proud of you!" I was, of course. Watching Sean move forward with his life filled me with joy. But the accompanying circumstances injected some unwanted negativity. Just at that moment, my phone rang. It was Rory. I wouldn't have answered any other call.

"Howdy, Pardner," he said.

"Huh?"

"I'm trying to get ready for Texas," Rory said.

Well of course he was! Rory was the best landscape architect in the business. That was how we had met, after all. Fifteen years before? I probably should have known Rory was involved in the Houston project. Perhaps I did. Perhaps I had never taken the whole thing seriously enough to consider all the players in it. Until I suddenly became the quarterback.

"Could I call you later?" I asked.

"Of course," Rory said. "Whenever."

I refocused my attention solely on Sean. "That was Rory," I said. "He thought I already knew, I guess. I'm not making sense. Sean, I was asked to helm a project in Houston today. I leave for Texas in about a week-and-a-half. And I just found out Rory will be there, too. He designed the public spaces. I should have known that. He's the best.

"Anyway, I thought I would be breaking the news to you, tonight, that *we're* heading to Houston soon. But, of course, everything has changed. You have your career plans and I have mine," I said. "I don't know how we're going to do this." The lump in my throat stopped me cold.

"I can start in the summer term," Sean said. "It won't matter."

"Fuck that!" I said. "You're starting your degree next week. That's the most important thing here. The rest is details." I didn't believe that, of course. But I put on a brave front. "Let's get something to eat. I can't make sense on an empty stomach." And that's what we did.

We barely spoke at all over our supper at my favorite neighborhood Japanese. But we smiled a lot. And I tried to stay up-beat. Sake helped. It wasn't until bedtime that I was able to break my silence. "This is going to be just fine," I said. "We'll share video calls every day, and I'll fly home to visit you now and then."

"Alex, I don't like this," he said. "We're supposed to be together."

"We *will* be together," I said without much conviction. "We'll just be 1,400 miles apart. When is spring break?"

"I didn't get that far."

"It doesn't matter. If it's early, then I'll fly you down to spend your break with me in Texas. And if it's in April, then I'll probably be home already. We'll make it work," I said with false conviction. There didn't seem to be any real way to lighten the situation.

But then I had an idea: "Get Mike to come and live with you here while I'm away. I don't want you alone, Sean. Tell him I'll pay his rent while he's here. How much could a walkup in Alphabet City cost? Don't answer that. Whatever it is, it'll be fine. I know it's getting late, but why don't you text him now? I'll sleep better if I know we're getting you settled."

Sean did as I asked. He received no reply for a while, but then just before lights out, Mike texted, "Sure." So, I did feel a bit better able to sleep. It was still a fitful night. Creepy dreams full of loss and violence. But whenever I shouted myself awake, Sean was still beside me. And I was determined to savor his presence for as long as possible.

📖

I didn't return Rory's call until noontime the next day. I didn't know what to say. Still, I had to tell him Sean was not going to Texas with me. "Don't worry, Alex. You won't be alone," Rory said. "You'll have me." That was true enough. Rory—and lots of work to do. How could loneliness stand a chance?

"But it feels so wrong, Rory," I said. "Sean just got here, and now I'm going to disappear for a few months? What a fuck-up."

"Hush, Alex," he said. "Sean worships you—as do I, of course—so everything will be just fine."

"I wish I could believe that."

"Believe!" he said. "Look, Alex, you're going to Texas to take advantage of an excellent career opportunity. And Sean is staying in New York to take advantage of an excellent career opportunity. There's no point in second-guessing the situation or the timing. It is what it is. And it's only for now. Not forever."

Maybe the rationality of Rory's argument talked me down from my ledge. Or maybe I had had enough of the drama of it all. Maybe I started to take an adult approach to the situation. As if that were possible. I told Rory, "Mike said he'll move into my apartment to keep Sean company while I'm away."

"Good. He's a sweet boy. And good company."

"Don't you want him with you?"

"It never occurred to me," Rory said. "My mind doesn't work that way."

"No, I suppose it doesn't," I said.

"But speaking of housing," Rory said, "the company got a good monthly rental deal on a furnished apartment near the building site. It has two bedrooms. I think you should take the second bedroom. Talk to the finance guys at your firm. I'm sure they'll want to share costs with us."

"You want me to live with you?" I asked.

"Sure. Why not?"

"Well, for starters, we have history, Rory," I said. "What if I have an extra scotch some night and decide I want to slip into your bed? I can imagine a situation like that without much of a stretch."

"We'll handle it," he said. "We always have, Alex. We know each other."

I felt I knew—and loved—every inch of my best friend. His dark beauty had mesmerized me for a big chunk of my adult life. He had never denied me access to the perfection of his body or the sweetness of his soul. His heart was a different matter, of course. But even that was partially mine. Surely.

"I don't know, Rory," I said. "I thought Sean and I would be—monogamous, I guess." It sounded creepy to my ears, and yet I had probably hoped that

I would be enough for Sean. Physically. Surely he was more than enough for me. Wasn't he?

"Are we complicating things here, Rory?" I asked. "You were a perfect friend to me when Sean disappeared. You slept in my bed and kept me from dying of loneliness, but you never touched me sexually. I would have welcomed your body any way you wanted to share it. But you knew that would have been the wrong way to prove your friendship. That was then. Now? I don't know, Rory. I can't see living with you for a few months in Texas without tasting you again. I don't think I'm capable of that."

"Are you maybe being a little dramatic, Alex?" he asked. "Are you saying you don't feel safe with me?"

"No, I would never say that. I've trusted you completely all the years we've known each other, Rory. I'm saying I don't always trust myself. What if ...?"

Rory said, "What happens in Houston stays in Houston."

I wasn't exactly thrilled with the diminished amount of time I got to spend with Bradley that winter. While he and Nina were setting up their new fitness business, he was unavailable to share dinner several nights a week. *Most* nights a week, really. Our first months together, since July, had been so unencumbered by concerns outside the nine-to-five.

But after Christmas, it seemed that I had to make an appointment to schedule quality time alone with my perfect mate. And more often than not, he was unavailable. I'm being dramatic, of course. Bradley brought his perfection home every night and slept in my bed—our bed—with his arms around me.

But it was different. Where before we had romped with reckless abandon and bounced around my bedroom like acrobats (Bradley actually *was* one, while I had come to feel like an acrobat when I was with him) we had become a rather staid partnered couple with responsibilities. Where I was used to hearing, "Fuck me, Daddy!" I was more likely to hear, "Are you okay, Daddy? I have to be up so early tomorrow, I can't believe it. I love you."

The "I love you" part was always precious, of course. And when Bradley started to snore softly, I knew that I was safe in his perfectly strong arms and that nothing bad could happen to me before morning. But it was quite different from where we had started—at Fire Island Pines, in July.

"Beau, you know it's what you wanted for Bradley," said Izzy, my best friend, at lunch one Monday in February. "And you knew it would take long hours."

"I just didn't think I would have to surrender *unfettered access* to the most glorious man in New York while he becomes even more glorious," I said. "I have *needs*, Izzy. As if you didn't know." Isamu Matsuda was my first love. And if he had been more available—more willing to commit to some mystical, unbreakable, eternal union of body and soul—we would most likely have remained together as mates rather than besties.

Our current relationship was precious to me. To Izzy, too, I'm sure. I was comfortable with that. And grateful. But did I have the occasional thoughts about what it would be like if Izzy and I were back together and fucking like the twenty-somethings we had been when we were dating? I didn't need a whole lot of reminders.

Izzy and I had made love in July, after all. The night before Bradley and I met. It was sweet. And hot. And tempting in a life-changing way. And yet, when Bradley appeared on the scene, there was no question of where I was headed. Izzy knew it, of course. He engineered Bradley's and my first night together, after all.

"Gerald hates me," I said, recalling how Bradley had been Gerald Cartwright's date that perfect summer holiday, and how I had slept with Bradley immediately after Gerald returned to the city on legal business. Izzy let loose with the silvery laughter that had seemed much too rare when we were dating. It isn't that he had giggled behind his hand like a Japanese schoolgirl. It was just that he reserved true mirth for selected occasions. When he did laugh—truly—it was like a burst of springtime that might have elicited blossoms on trees. It certainly made my sap rise.

"Gerald loves you more than he loves any of the rest of us," Izzy said. "Surely you know that."

"No, not really," I said.

"That's odd, Beau. I thought you knew."

"What?"

"If Gerald were capable of a committed, long-term relationship—which he is not—he would have chosen you years ago. He adores you, Beau. How could you not know that?"

How, indeed? I didn't think our little family-of-choice had such mysteries in it. I only knew that Izzy and I had fallen in love more than a decade before, that Pete and Louis were solid friends, that everyone had been to bed with Gerald at least three times, and that Bradley was welcomed into the family unequivocally the instant I fell in love with him.

But Gerald as my not-so-secret admirer? That took a bit of processing. I respected the fact that we had built a solid friendship on the remnants of a disappointing affair. I admired Gerald's legal expertise. I was very much aware that the mere thought of Gerald always gave me an erection. And I was deeply grateful that Gerald had set up the investment deal that would allow Bradley and Nina to create the fitness enterprise of their dreams.

But Gerald as a man who adored *me* above all other men? He certainly had strange ways of showing it. Or perhaps not. Perhaps I lacked perception.

Perhaps I was just entirely too stupid. And yet, I had earned the love of a few good men, including the most precious personal trainer on God's green Earth.

Just when I was starting to give up on the possibility of easiness in my future, Bradley said to me, "Daddy, Nina and I are going to take alternate Sundays off. I'm going first. Will you spend the day with me? I've missed you so much I can't stand it."

That was all I really needed, of course. The promise of Bradley in my arms, Bradley in my sight, Bradley within touching and tasting distance for an entire day. Perhaps I'd stop whimpering and start earning the right to call him my perfect mate. Mating has reciprocal responsibilities, after all. I wouldn't be any good for Bradley if I continued on the path toward becoming a petulant sniveler.

We made love as soon as we woke on Sunday morning. It was ... glorious, actually. It wasn't that I had forgotten the taste and the feel of Bradley or the exquisite warmth inside his body when I inhabited him. It was just that I had become like a man on the edge of death from starvation and thirst who suddenly arrives at an oasis.

Do I sound a bit too dramatic? It was exactly how I felt that quiet Sunday morning in February. The bedroom heater purred so softly that mostly all I could hear was the sound of Bradley's breathing. Once we had shared an exquisite explosion and our bodily functions began to normalize, I rested my head on Bradley's perfect chest. And then all I could hear was his heartbeat.

"You make beautiful music," I said to him.

"It's all for you, Daddy," he said.

"Could you face a little breakfast?" I asked.

"With you, I can face anything," he said. After another deep kiss, we threw on some robes and headed to the kitchen. I made coffee the way I usually do, and I brought out the croissants I had bought the day before. I popped them into the toaster-oven for a few minutes, and then I set them on the table with butter and the guava preserves Nina's mother had given us for Christmas. I looked in the fridge for the *dulce de leche* that had come with the fruit gift until I remembered Bradley and I had polished off the milk sweet in January.

We smiled a lot over breakfast. Smiled and munched and sipped good coffee with hot milk. I hadn't felt so warm and snuggly since before Christmas. My proximity to Bradley's perfect self kept me in a state of perpetual arousal. "You work out a lot of hot guys, every day, Bradley," I said. "How often do they give you an erection?" I instantly regretted the question, but it was too late to take it back. Life doesn't work that way.

"Often, Daddy," he said. "But so what? You're the only man I love, and the only man I need." Good answer! That earned Bradley a deep kiss and a return to our bed. It was almost like our honeymoon days at Fire Island. Always something new to discover. Always something new to savor.

That Sunday morning I became obsessed with Bradley's armpits. I had met them before, of course, but perhaps I had overlooked some of their beauty— the sculptural perfection of the muscles that defined them, the prettiness of the tufts of chestnut hair that tickled my nose, and the deeply individual musk that greeted my tongue.

I began to weep softly as I savored the unhurried perfection of a Sunday morning in bed with the man I loved. We graduated from exploration to full-on appetite. Everything about Bradley—not least of which was the fact that he seemed to feel the same way—made me shiver with desire.

"What can I do for my perfect baby boy?" I asked him.

"Just love me, Daddy," he said. "That's all I need." On the surface, that seemed a simple request. But *Of those to whom much is given, much is expected,* I pondered. Surely I had a responsibility to give Bradley exquisite gifts of my attention and my love. I began to doubt if I was enough. But when Bradley and I had shared an almost gentle orgasm, I put aside my fears. For then.

We didn't do much with the rest of the day— purely by design. We sipped coffee, later graduating to wine. We kissed a lot. We snacked on leftovers, and then later, we ordered in a Thai supper. We never bothered to dress. It didn't seem necessary. I'd have been content for both of us to stay nude for the entire day, but it was February, after all. There was a sprinkling of residual snow in the tree boxes visible from the front window. Nude would have seemed odd, even though the apartment was toasty enough. We settled for open robes. No extra layers of fabric to come between me and my man.

We read *The New York Times*—partially, at least. We talked. A lot. Bradley had been too tired most nights when he got home to share much about his business journey. He brought me up to speed on the plans he and Nina were making with Izzy's guidance and Gerald's legal advice.

"Daddy, Nina and I are working so hard to make this happen. To make a future. I just want you to be proud of me. I just want to make you happy."

I grabbed Bradley and pressed his glorious chest to mine. "Baby, every breath you take fills me with pride and happiness," I said. "You don't have to *do* anything. You don't have to *say* anything. You just have to *be*! That's all the Universe expects of you, and I couldn't ask for more."

I was haunted by what Izzy had told me about Gerald, and so I decided to investigate a little. Bradley was so focused on his work, and I seemed so filled with free time by comparison. I invited Gerald to lunch the following Thursday. He accepted. "It seems like a lifetime ago—when we met," I said as soon as we had ordered wine.

"It seems like yesterday to me," he replied. "But wait a few years, Beau—until you're my age—and everything will begin to feel like it was yesterday."

"Is that really the way it works?" I asked.

"Uh-huh. And time moves faster, too. You'll see. A year can go by in the twinkling of an eye."

"So much to look forward to," I said, without mirth. "What were we talking about?"

"You were going to ask me about Bradley and Thanksgiving."

"Right. When he asked you why you were helping him and Nina to get their fitness empire off the ground, you told him it was the only gift you could give him that would last. Or something like that. Did I get it right?"

"Almost," Gerald said. "I told him his happiness was important to me. And since he had found you, Beau, the only other gift he needed was a leg-up in business."

"I know you're always honest with me, Gerald," I said. "Is that the whole truth?"

Gerald looked thoughtful, and he chose his words carefully. "Nearly. There's also the matter of you, Beau. I also did it for you. You're probably feeling like a work widow at the moment, but you'll thank me one day, Beau, when Bradley's business is secure and he has more time to devote to you. He will, you know. Bradley worships you. Any fool could see that."

"I'm feeling a little off balance," I said. "Nothing new when I'm around you. Why me, Gerald? I doubt you keep a log of your conquests, but I'm guessing there have been thousands. Why me?"

"It goes all the way back to the day we met, at the Foundation. You had the sweetest smile when you greeted me, Beau. It was hard to concentrate on the meeting, but I managed to represent my client properly. And then I could focus on what I really wanted to do that day. That's why I asked you for directions to the men's room. I knew you would guide me."

"And then you pushed me into a stall and humped me like a savage."

"It was fun, wasn't it?"

"One of my happiest memories," I answered honestly.

"You were the prettiest thing I'd ever seen, Beau. Still are. I wanted you in the worst way. And that's how I got you. There was no protest, as I remember."

"None," I said. "I was too shocked. I had never met a man who saw something he wanted and just took it. Bradley is the only other man who has ever wanted me so totally, but he has a very different way of showing it. I remember every moment we shared in bed, Gerald. Unfortunately, I remember the post-coital cold shoulder as clearly as the passion."

"I'm not made for love, Beau. You've known that for a long time."

"Yes. Fortunately, you have other skills."

"You mean legal skills, don't you?" he asked.

"That too," I said. "You know this menu, Gerald. What should I order?" And so we sipped our wine and ordered some interesting winter lunchy salady things and retired the subject of Gerald's passion for me. But like Jesus's mother, I kept those things in my heart.

📖

When Bradley got home from work that night—much too late, as far as I was concerned, as always—he said, as we were getting ready for bed, "Nina has a client who's new to the city. He's single and doesn't want to be. She says he's a quality guy, and he's crazy about Asian men. Her first thought was that this guy should meet Izzy. I agree, but I wanted to discuss it with you."

"Bradley, you have an enormous ... heart," I said. "But matchmaking is tricky at best."

"Well, if anyone can manage it, it's you, Daddy," Bradley said.

"I'll see what I can do," I said just before we kissed and snuggled and settled into our places on the Dreamland Express. Hmmm. Izzy. Partnered. After all these years. A worthy goal, surely. Could I accomplish such a feat? Would I even want to? Why not?

Just before Bradley left for work in the morning—much too early, as always—I said to him, "I wish I could stage a little dinner party, but you and Nina are never free. So, get me a dinner date with this client of hers, on some pretext or other. I'll have to screen him. I can't just throw him at Izzy without vetting him first!"

"Thanks, Daddy," Bradley said. And sure enough, he called me at lunchtime to tell me that Nina's client, Roger Willard, had two tickets for the opera the following evening and needed a date. "I sort of volunteered you, Daddy. If you don't want to go, just tell me. But it seemed like a perfect opportunity for you to meet him."

"Yes, Baby," I said. "A perfect coincidence. What's the opera?"

"He didn't say."

"I just wondered how long it is. If it's one with an 8:00 curtain, then maybe we can meet for an early supper before. But, it doesn't matter, Baby. I'll meet him whenever he likes. Give him my contact info. I'll leave work a little early if necessary."

"Thanks, Daddy!"

"No, wait, Baby. I've been so stupid! The Foundation knows people at the Grand Tier Restaurant at the Met. I'm sure I can get us a table. So we can start dinner before the curtain and then go back for more courses during intermissions. I'll have to dress up a little, but if we find Izzy the perfect mate, it will be worth it."

"I love you, Daddy," Bradley said. "Gotta go!" And so that's how I found myself scheduled to hear *Turandot* at the Metropolitan Opera the following evening. I was glad I had a clean—and pressed—dress shirt in my closet.

Turandot is a remarkable opera, of course, and the Met's production—one of the glorious holdovers from that golden age in the 80s and early 90s when Franco Zeffirelli created stagings that were breathtaking and irreplaceable—is always a memorable evening in the theater. I hoped that Roger would measure up to the occasion.

We met at the restaurant on the mezzanine. He was early. I was only five minutes late. We shook hands, smiled a lot, ordered some wine, and said the usual pleasantries that people try to share when they are on their best behavior. Mostly, of course, I was sizing Roger up.

He was medium height, with a tight, fit little body quite evident under his well-cut suit. I also liked his face. I guess I'd call it ... open? Or, endearing, maybe? Handsome, for sure. Smoky-blue eyes. Generous lashes. And a smile that could melt ice cubes as well as hearts, I surmised.

"What brings you to New York?" I asked him.

"I've wanted to live here ever since I was a little boy," he said. I began to imagine Roger as a little boy—an exceptionally beautiful little boy, no doubt.

I imagined a chipped front tooth that had to be repaired later. That was the only flaw I could conjure up for him.

"I almost went to Columbia," he said, "but my parents wanted me to study at Northwestern. I gave in. And then Wharton for my MBA. The folks were willing to pay for that. A few decent jobs, and now I'm here!"

"Well, New York City doesn't have a welcoming committee anymore," I said, "but I, for one, am delighted you're here."

"Thanks, Beau. I'm so glad I found Nina and Bradley. They're both amazing. Nina seems to know what my body needs before I do. She's not easy, of course, but I feel safe in her hands."

"Exactly," I said. "No, she's not easy. But what would be the point in that?"

"Beau, I have to say how much I envy your relationship with Bradley. I hope you'll forgive me for telling you this, but you have what I want. I've been looking for a love like that, with a quality man. I don't expect it to be easy, any more than I expect a relationship with a quality trainer to be easy. But I want it with all my heart."

It was that kind of evening. The food was quite good at the Grand Tier, the singing was even better. The golden glow of the Zeffirelli *Turandot* mesmerized us, as always. And by the time Roger and I were headed toward home and saying good-night with a slightly-less-than-chaste kiss, I was satisfied that Roger had passed the screening process with flying colors.

📖

Bradley had already turned in when I got home from my opera evening. I stripped and hung up my suit—the good navy blue one that I rarely have the need or the occasion or the *will* to wear anymore. Then I brushed my teeth and headed to bed as quietly as possible. A part of me wanted a chat and a nightcap and a kiss. The angels of my better nature urged me to be still and considerate. Bradley needed his well-earned rest, after all.

To be fair to myself, I must say that Bradley always knew when I was present, especially if I was restless or I coughed or I had a dream that made me twitch or if I got up to pee in the night. No detail of my existence seemed to escape his eyes even when they were somnolent. So even though Bradley was snoring softly and I slipped into bed that night with commendable grace, he knew I was there.

When Bradley put his arms around me, I suddenly felt that I was truly home. "Did he solve the riddle?" Bradley asked.

"What?"

"There's a riddle, isn't there?" Bradley asked sleepily.

"Oh, yes, three of them, actually. But then Calàf turns it back on Turandot and makes her guess his name."

"How did she do tonight?" Bradley asked without really opening his eyes.

"She was splendid," I said. "But, really, I could have told her. He has the same name as you, Baby. His name is Love." Bradley gripped me. I started to weep softly. Could I then have gone quietly to sleep? Maybe. Bradley knew better.

"Daddy needs a brandy," Bradley said. "Follow me." He made a sort of dancelike move that got him gracefully out of bed and over to my side, where he took my hand and led me to the kitchen. And there he poured me a stiff cognac and a splash for himself. Bradley stood behind me and began to massage my shoulders. That was heavenly, but the way his perfect cock began to rise between my legs was even more celestial.

"Baby needs his sleep," I said. "This is no time to unleash the beast."

"It's okay, Daddy," he said. "There's time for everything. So, what did you think of Roger? He's cute, isn't he?"

"Very," I said.

"Will Izzy agree?"

"We'll find out soon enough," I said. "I think they'd be perfect together, Roger and Izzy, but it's not up to me. Still, I'll do my part and cook up some scheme to get them together. In fact, I'll start tomorrow." A quick glance at the kitchen clock led me to amend that statement: "*Today*, as it happens. Come on Baby, let's get you to bed. It's so late."

Bradley finished his massage work on my shoulders, turned me around, and kissed me deeply. I was completely under his spell and would still be kissing Bradley if he hadn't paused long enough to suggest that we adjourn to the bedroom.

I tucked Bradley in, and by the time I had made it to my side of the bed, he had already slipped into his signature nighttime breathing right on the edge of a gentle snore. It was music to my ears.

"Do you love me?" I asked Izzy at lunch the next day.

"Don't be silly, Beau. You know I do. Have for more than a decade—isn't it? Why do you ask?"

"Because I'm not satisfied with your life, the way it's going."

Izzy studied me with a quizzical look before replying, "So my big White brother has all the answers, is that it?" I was stunned, of course. Izzy and I had never actually quarreled. Not even when we were uncoupling. *Especially* not then. I think we both knew we were making choices we might live to regret.

"I want you partnered, Izzy, that's all. I want you to have what Bradley and I share. I'm not going to say that I want you to have what *you and I* could have shared if you had wanted it. That's part of it, of course. But let's drop the past and talk about the future."

"I know you mean well, Beau, but aren't you over-stepping some boundaries here? My bed is my business."

"I'm talking about your *life*, Izzy. And your heart. And your future. There's someone I want you to meet, Iz. I think he could be good for you. I think you could invest a few hours in finding out. I think a date wouldn't kill you."

"Look, Beau, I can find my own dates," he said.

"Apparently not," I said before I had a chance to unthink that response. "I mean, I want you to be happy, Iz. I want you to have dinner with this guy and take him home and fuck him silly and fall so deeply in love with him that your life is upended. I want you to let go, Izzy. Drop the armor. Will you at least try it?" Izzy seemed thoughtful. That was something, anyway. I vowed to shut up and wait.

Before long, Izzy said, "Beau, I've never really been angry with you. You're too precious for that. If you want me to meet this guy, then I'll meet him. But please don't ever do this to me again!" I reached across the table and took Izzy's hands in mine.

I thought, *My, that went well, didn't it?* There wasn't really anything more to say. Izzy knew that I would arrange a mutually convenient time for him to meet Roger. And I knew they would have a pleasant evening together, at the very least. But I had a sudden twinge around the heart as I realized that I was giving Izzy away!

Tale Number Seven

In case you haven't guessed it already, I'll admit that I did reach out to Jeremy. It wasn't immediately, though. I told Morgan I wasn't yet ready to invite Jeremy to come home. She assured me that she would be in New York through January before leaving to start her new fellowship at UC Berkeley. That gave me some wiggle room until after Christmas.

I doubt either Morgan or I believed Jeremy was so fragile that he couldn't survive on his own—for a day or a month or a year or forever. It was just that we both loved him so deeply that the idea of leaving him to fend for himself seemed a nonstarter. Morgan had only loved Jeremy for most of that year. My obsession reached back to when I was not quite fifteen, when he was my history teacher.

Had we not run into each other by chance about six years ago—on MacDougal Street in the Village—I would never have known that Jeremy had taken a teaching post at NYU, and he would never have known that I had been living in the neighborhood since college.

I chuckled to myself thinking about how quickly Jeremy and I had made up for lost time. We were living together within a week of that chance meeting.

And instantly, I think, we both knew that our lives were finally on course. There was no room for doubt until suddenly there was.

If Morgan hadn't joined the History Department as a teaching assistant the previous spring, and if she hadn't been so bright and capable and pretty and vulnerable to Jeremy's considerable charms, would my relationship have gone from my rock to on-the-rocks? *That* was the question that perplexed me.

Shit happens. Mates stray. I'm not stupid. I don't have a Pollyanna bone in my body. Maybe. But I kept thinking, *How could he? After all we've been through! After all the years we were apart—and then finding each other again by chance and starting the shared lives we were always meant to have!*

That was the anger surfacing, of course. But the deeper pain was of the *Why am I not enough?* variety. If Jeremy had said at dinner one night, "We need more dick in our lives. I have a student who's keen to bed me. Us, actually. You met him at that mixer, Wally. He thinks you're super hot. So obviously he has great taste. What do you think?" I might have said, "Bring him on!"

Maybe. I liked to believe I was capable of a the-more-the-merrier mentality when it comes to sex. Do I believe that variety is the spice of life? No, actually. But I get it. I'd have been willing to go to an orgy with Jeremy if it brought him pleasure. Maybe. But this situation was so fucking different!

I guess I'm saying that affairs of the crotch seem rather simple to me, while affairs of the heart I sometimes find deeply complex. So if I wasn't quite ready to welcome Jeremy back into my life and into my heart and into my bed—our bed?—then perhaps you'll understand why.

When my best friend invited me to spend Thanksgiving with his family, I declined. I knew it would be a warm, festive day. I had happy memories of spending a holiday or two with Ryan Chatterjee and his family in Pennsylvania back when we were dating. But I wasn't ready to accept a stand-in for the celebration Jeremy and I should have shared. I preferred to spend the day alone—with Chinese takeout and Netflix. It was tolerable.

When my mother phoned, I told her that Jeremy and I would be heading out to a friend's for an early dinner. She didn't ask me to put Jeremy on the phone. I knew she wouldn't, so there was no need to prepare any additional lies. I didn't ask her what she and Dad were doing that day. I assumed my parents were still together. I assumed their trial separation was something from my teen years that they outgrew.

At the time, I had assumed it was my fault, of course. That's what kids do. I had suffered great guilt pangs for being such a failure as a son that I destroyed their marriage. Anyone who's ever been to that neighborhood will understand completely. And the rest of you will please take my word for it. But by the time I reached my early thirties, I didn't much care, really. I had maybe worked my way past most of that bitterness and disappointment. Maybe.

I had lunch the following Monday with Ryan. The little Turkish restaurant near the office was inviting, as always. It was a crisp, clear day, and we sat near the front window. A shaft of crystalline sunlight illuminated Ryan, as if it were merely intensifying the light that shone from within him. Everything about him sparkled—his raven hair, his creamy skin, his perfect teeth, the golden flecks in his dreamy eyes that always made me think of a tiger with clear ideas about how best to eat me.

I thought, *How many times have I made love to this beauty?* There were the years we were dating—just before Jeremy and I rediscovered each other. And in recent months there had been those weekends that Ryan spent with me. How many times had he held me and rescued me from bleak loneliness? How many times had he made me laugh and assured me that life is beautiful? How many times had he filled my body with the generous perfection of his own?

Mostly, of course, I wondered how I could love Ryan so deeply and still want Jeremy more. Ah, there was the rub! At lunch, Ryan said to me, "You know, Christmas is only a few weeks away, *mera an-amol*. You could come home with me. Mama would love to have you. And so would I." I had mostly accepted that I was precious to Ryan, but his Hindi terms of endearment always made me teary.

"What's a Hindu Christmas feast like?" I asked.

"Pretty much like Thanksgiving," he said. That conjured up memories of warmth and spice and welcome—the sort of holiday everyone is supposed to experience but that my family of origin lacked the skill to pull off. Or the will. Can't say which. I accepted Ryan's invitation.

I was waiting in the lobby when Ryan's sister Aniya drove up in front of my building on the morning of Christmas Eve. Packing had been quick and easy, after all. I only needed a change of underwear, a clean T, and a few toiletries—plus the little gifts I had bought for Ryan and his mother. Once I had tossed it all into my favorite leather backpack, I was all set.

We exchanged the usual greetings, and I slipped into the back seat of Aniya's BMW. The family resemblance between Ryan and Aniya was uncanny. They could only have been siblings. From my comfortable perch in the back seat, I could see both of them clearly as they interacted. As only siblings can. I had a brief fantasy—a *very* brief fantasy—where I imagined the three of us making love together. And then I nodded off to sleep, but not before I decided that I was unwilling to share Ryan with anyone!

I napped most of the way to Pennsylvania—like a cat stretched out on a sunny sofa. As Aniya's car purred into the wide suburban driveway, I roused myself in time for Mrs. Chatterjee's greeting. "It's lovely to see you again, Walla. We're delighted to have you here. Please come in!" I grabbed my bag— and Aniya's—and followed my hosts dutifully up the walkway to the front door.

Mr. Chatterjee was waiting for us in the foyer. He greeted his children warmly. I received a rather stiff handshake, as if I were some remnant of the Raj best forgotten. Or so I imagined. I was not proud of the conclusion I had drawn. Surely I could have felt a little compassion for a man reared in a traditional society faced with welcoming his son's male lover into his home. Or ex-lover? I wasn't certain which.

Mrs. Chatterjee, however, was all charm and hospitality. "Walla, you must come and sit by the fire. You can take your bag up later. Did I show you Ryan's baby pictures? I probably did. What a pretty child he was. Nearly as pretty as Aniya," she added out of fairness. I remembered my gift and reached into my bag to retrieve it.

"Mrs. Chatterjee," I said. "This scent made me think of you. I hope you like it." I had bought her a French *eau de parfum* spray based on warm spices with primary notes of mango and vanilla (or base notes? What do I know about perfume?). She embraced me sweetly and kissed me on the cheek.

"I'm sure I'll love it," she said. "Come, everyone. Let's warm you up!" We dutifully went to sit by the fire, of course. I couldn't help watching Ryan and Aniya interacting with their parents. I might just as well have grown up on another planet, so different was my experience of family.

It didn't matter how often Aniya rolled her eyes when her mother said something with veiled negativity about her daughter's unmarried state. And it didn't matter that Ryan sometimes seemed to clench his jaw muscles when his father lectured him on the fine points of business. All that mattered was their love for each other.

I melted into the welcoming warmth of being part of a family. And then Mrs. Chatterjee opened my gift and said, "Walla, this is perfect!" She proceeded to add a little spritz here and there to lampshades around the room. And within a few minutes we were enveloped in a transparent cloud of spiced comfort. In fact, the whole house suddenly smelled like Christmas!

Luncheon was simple, and then Ryan and I put on our coats and gloves and went for a walk around the grounds. The stillness of the frigid air allowed for that phenomenon where each breath seems to crackle as it frosts nose hairs and tickles the lining of the lungs. Add that to the crunch of footfalls in patches of residual snow and experience the best that winter has to offer.

Ryan and I locked arms and walked down the hill toward the little stream. "It will most likely freeze over soon," he said. "See the ice forming around the edges? I've never understood how the frogs survive the cold here. But each spring they're back—croaking and singing as if nothing had happened to shut them down."

"Ryan, I think you could be quite happy living here," I said.

"I could be quite happy living anywhere with … the right man," he said. "And I don't have to tell you who he is." I had a sudden compulsion to kiss Ryan. Deeply. I resisted the urge. It didn't seem fair. I never seemed able to give him what he really needed. What he deserved. So, Ryan initiated our kiss. As always, he settled for what I had to offer him.

We've all heard of burning kisses, of course, but that Christmas Eve, early in winter's chill, Ryan's mouth seared mine with an intensity that turned my core molten as it sent my dick into full extension. It frightened me, really. I had never actually been frightened by an unexpected kiss—except for the first one, probably, when my freshman college roommate took a sudden interest in me.

I savored Ryan's kiss for as long as I dared. Surely we would be expected at the house for dinner soon. Surely someone would walk down the hill and discover us. Surely the bliss of the moment couldn't last. I ended our kiss. Reluctantly. "I don't know what to say."

"Then don't say anything," Ryan suggested. The spell was broken. The moment had ended. We wandered rather aimlessly back up to the house. There wasn't much that needed doing before dinner, but I took my bag to the upstairs bedroom Mrs. Chatterjee had assigned me. Ryan showed me the way.

"It's a comfortable bed, Wally," he said, "but I want you to sleep with me tonight."

"Yes, please. Wherever you say."

"Then let's sleep in my bed. It's small, but I think we'll be safe if you hold on tight."

"That was my intention," I said. And then Ryan kissed me. It was a very sweet kiss, but it lacked the urgency and the heat level of our earlier kiss, on the lawn. I feared I had—yet again—screwed up my relationship with Ryan, simply because I couldn't quite get my heart right. Would I ever sort it out? Who the fuck knew?

Christmas Eve dinner was elaborate, by anyone's standards, I think. As it happened, Mrs. Chatterjee had once had an Italian American neighbor who impressed her with the breadth and savor of her "Seven Fishes" ritual. Not one to be outdone, Ila Chatterjee had created a seafood feast of her own. And the results were bordering on magnificent!

There were kingfish and prawns and Atlantic blue crabs from not that far down the Delaware River and other water creatures in season. Each preparation was perfectly realized, bursting with flavor, and completely different from all the others. One savory explosion after another, and nothing that said "curry."

I was abuzz with contentment and the residual heat of chiles permeating my entire digestive system when Ryan and I thanked his parents for the feast and headed upstairs. "Should I mess up the bed a little?" I asked as we retrieved my bag from the guest room and headed to Ryan's.

"I forget sometimes how Southern you are," he said. And then Ryan laughed at me. It was golden laughter, like a blessing from the heavens (whatever and wherever they are). I couldn't quite remember when I had felt so light and free—despite a very full belly. He laughed at me! The man I loved more than life, at that particular moment, found me amusing!

"Accident of birth," I said. "Could we please go to bed?"

"Of course, *meree aatma.*" I sensed that actually Ryan had become *my* soul. And I began to wonder how I could ever face the future without the two of us together as one. And yet, surely, I had had those same feelings when Jeremy and I combined our lives. Had them still, to be honest.

When we got to Ryan's room, I put my bag down and took my toiletries to the bathroom. I was trying to be an organized guest, I suppose. Or trying to find a hint of normality in the ritual of preparing for sleep. And then I returned to see Ryan turning down the bed. It was a nice room. A few school pennants and posters on the walls, of course, all carefully curated by his mother.

I had seen Aniya's room on a previous visit. Too pink and frilly, perhaps, but inescapably a reflection of her past. I wondered what my mother had done with *my* room. But that was a fleeting thought. Because I was so fucking glad to have escaped the confines of it that I had never really looked back. Or not for more than a few moments. And certainly not in anger. Maybe.

I reached into my bag and took out my Christmas gift for Ryan. I had chosen a puffy heart carved from Tiger Eye and edged in gold. I was a little nervous about my choice, because Ryan didn't wear much jewelry except for the pinky ring I gave him when we were dating. But I had seen the Tiger Eye pendant in a jewelry store and known that I would have to buy it for him.

"Wally, this is so lovely! But we said no gifts!" That was true enough. "I don't have a gift for you!"

"*You* are a gift for me!" I said. "Could I have a kiss?" And of course Ryan gave me the kiss I craved. And then he went to the little box on his chest of drawers and took out a delicate gold chain. He threaded my gift onto the chain and fastened it around his neck. The pendant fell right into the divot between his collar bones.

It was perfect, of course. Nearly as perfect as Ryan himself. I eased us toward bed and lights-out in the hope of hiding my tears. I loved spending the night with Ryan in his boyhood bed. It was small, but when Ryan held me in his strong arms, it felt like a perfect fit.

"Merry Christmas, *mera jeevan*," Ryan said as he snuggled close. Yes, he had offered me the chance to be his life. Many times. But I had never accepted the responsibility. Could I maybe make sense of it all in the new year? But that Christmas Eve, all I could manage was to accept Ryan's warmth and his kiss and his body filling mine with love and safety.

　

"It's Mother's version of kedgeree," Ryan said the next morning at breakfast. He was pointing at a strange dish that looked—and smelled—rather like fish and rice. "The scrambled eggs are always safe." Ryan looked like heaven-on-toast, as far as I was concerned. He was still wearing my gift. It looked even better in daylight than it had looked at midnight. I had always marveled at how Ryan could slip out of bed in the morning, run his fingers through his hair, and resemble the Hindu version of Apollo.

It was an English breakfast, meaning that it was a buffet where we were all expected to fend for ourselves whenever we chose to show up. Within reason, of course. Ryan and I came downstairs around 9:00, I think. Aniya wandered in, sleepily, just as I was about to consider seconds. "You boys look well rested," she said. "Someone had a visit from Santa, I see. Well, Bro, isn't this something to be discussed with the family?"

"Everyone in this family knows how much I adore Wally," Ryan said, "so I think we've already had that discussion." Had they? Had any of us sorted any of it? Mrs. Chatterjee breezed in to kiss her children, and then she breezed back to the kitchen. She and her helpers had more important things to deal with than breakfast! Mr. Chatterjee, who had breakfasted hours before, popped in to wish us all a good morning. He also greeted his daughter with a kiss. And then he greeted his son with a kiss.

Bruce K Beck

Fuck! I thought. *How different would my life be if my father loved me?* And suddenly I was sitting with the remnants of my Christmas breakfast wondering if my father had ever loved me. Surely I had wanted his love. Surely I had adored him when I was a child. And, just as surely, we had disappointed each other at every turn.

"Did you try the gooseberry jam?" Ryan asked. "It's quite wonderful." He put his hand on my thigh. His nearly imperceptible squeeze told me that he was right there with me, that he could carry me and my pain whenever I needed to climb onto his beautiful shoulders, and that he would never let me down. But what had *I* to offer *him*?

It was a quiet day. Ryan and I slipped on our coats and drove into town to get something Mrs. Chatterjee needed from the only store in town that was open on Christmas Day. Then we took a nap—the best part of it for me because Ryan held me in his arms the whole time. And then we showered to-gether, just as we had done when we were boyfriends. And then we dressed and went to the dining room for the big event.

Mrs. Chatterjee's turkey masala was just as sa-vory as I remembered. And her famous pumpkin treacle pudding with ginger sauce gave the crowning touch to our feast. It even had a gold-leaf crown! I had—quite honestly—only felt that kind of holiday joy once before: also at the Chatterjees'. When Ryan and I were dating.

Mr. Chatterjee shot me a few sidelong glances—maybe. He also poured wine and offered me choice bits from the turkey platter. Anya took me aside while her mother was preparing her special holiday spiced tea. She pulled me out onto the side porch—

where she could light a cigarette without excessive disapproval—and said, "Wally, you've grown even better looking than when you and Ry were dating. How did you manage that?"

"The same way you managed to become the biggest heartbreaker in the Northeast," I said. "Ryan tells me about the trail of tears that follows your rejects. I used to think you had a heart."

"I did," she said and took a deep drag from her cigarette. "But I gave it to you, Wally. It seems to be a family trait." I had no answer for that, so I embraced Aniya instead of speaking. Even though she shared all of Ryan's warmth, much of his strength, and most of his beauty, I sensed we were headed for a conversation I was not going to like.

"Look, Wally," she said, "you know I worship my big brother."

"So do I," I interjected.

Aniya sized up that comment with a healthy dose of skepticism and said, "I think he's getting his hopes up again. I don't want to see him hurt. Again. I don't think you wound him on purpose. But if you can't love him, Wally, then just stay away from him!"

That felt like a gut punch. I had always thought of myself as a fairly nice guy to whom things and people happen. But suddenly I had to consider myself as a player in someone else's life—for good or for ill. That might take some reconsideration.

"I'm doing the best I can here, Aniya," I said. "I care more about Ryan's happiness than about my own. But my heart is obsessed with a man I've known since I was a teenager. If Jeremy didn't exist, I'd have asked Ryan to marry me years ago. But I can't give your precious brother the devotion he deserves."

I was sort of winging it there. And I wondered how honest I had been. I wondered if I had it in my power to excise Jeremy from my heart and to get on with the possibility of sharing my life with Ryan. Surely removing Jeremy would be an invasive and bloody procedure. I doubt they make an anesthesia for that.

Aniya tamped out her cigarette, studied my face, and kissed me rather sweetly. And then she said, "Let's go in. Mama's tea is surely ready. I'll slip you some brandy to spike it. Wally," she said, "grow up!" I knew instantly I deserved that. I also knew I had no idea how to go about it.

Christmas night in Ryan's little bed felt safe and peaceful. I hated having to disentangle our limbs in the morning. I wasn't ready to give up the holiday magic, but it was surely time to break the spell. As we piled into Aniya's car—now stuffed with leftovers and jars of mango preserves—there was no question we were headed back to reality.

Ryan knew I would be calling Jeremy. "You can handle this, Wally," he told me at the office the following week. I was less certain, I suppose. It was the most complicated situation of my life. Falling in love with Jeremy when I was still a kid seemed simple in comparison—despite the impossibility of our student/teacher dynamic. Back then, there was nothing to be done. I finished high school. Jeremy got out of town—not out of guilt, really, because there was none, but out of an abundance of caution. Plus a dose of self-preservation.

But after our chance reunion—nearly six years ago—life had begun to feel rather perfect. Until it didn't anymore. Life had seemed perfect until Jeremy began to come home late and distracted. Until Jeremy came home smelling of someone else. And when that someone else turned out to be a very handsome, accomplished, young *woman*—Jeremy's mentee, really—life grew decidedly imperfect.

I had good reasons for proposing a meeting with Jeremy. Or so I hoped. He hadn't exactly left me, after all. Rather, we had agreed that he should go and stay with two colleagues until he could sort out his heart. But then Morgan did it for him. When she met me for coffee and asked me to take Jeremy back—because she was leaving New York but refused to have Jeremy remain alone—it began to seem inevitable that I *would* take him back. Maybe.

Morgan was so convinced that Jeremy and I belong together—so certain that her affair with Jeremy was wrong for both of them—that I began to believe in her wisdom. Or was there a healthy measure of wishful thinking involved? It was the first week in January when I phoned Jeremy and suggested we meet for a drink after work some evening soon.

"How about tonight?" he asked.

"Sure." I was nearly as nervous as a schoolboy before the prom. Only, Jeremy already knew every inch of me, inside and out, at my best and at my worst. So there was nothing I could hide. Nothing I could try to enhance.

Once we had met, shared a brief kiss, and ordered drinks, Jeremy said, "You look great, Wally. Winter always makes you sparkle."

"That sounds like a song lyric," I said. "And I think you got the wrong season. But I'll accept the compliment. I like the beard, Jeremy. Now you really do look like a history professor."

"Well, that's who I am," he said. "Things have changed. I used to be the partner of the most precious man on Earth."

"Thanks, Jeremy, but I don't think I can handle that," I said.

"Fair enough. Morgan told me she asked you ..."

"Yes, she did," I said. "And that's because she loves you. No surprise there."

"I don't know, Wally. I don't know what's right here. I know that I've loved you with my whole heart since you were a teen and I was a very unhappy twenty-something, and I know I fucked up. I can't really explain my feelings for Morgan, but I know you deserve better than a man who goes off on a tangent. I want us back together. But I have no right to ask you for that gift."

"Thanks for your honesty," I said. "I know this isn't any easier for you than it is for me, Jeremy."

"My future is in your hands, Wally. Just tell me what you want."

What, indeed? Did I invite Jeremy home? No. Would I? Probably. But not that night. A trial recoupling? Probably. The mere idea of it seemed creepy, and yet I couldn't imagine any other way to pick up the pieces and resume our lives.

"Bill and Charley won't mind if you stay with them for a while longer, will they?" I asked.

"No, they're fine with it."

"Good," I said. "Let's stick with that for now." I rose to leave. Jeremy paid the check and met me on the sidewalk. When he took me in his arms, it felt both natural and surprising, as if some alien presence had appeared where once we had been merely two people perfectly attuned.

"Wally, I love you so much!" he said.

So much that it hurts? I thought. *Sounds right.* When I kissed Jeremy, I started to get a little weepy. Every sinew in my body wanted to weave itself around his. Every organ, every gland sought the matching warmth of his. Surely that was how we had been. Before. And now?

"Call me next week," I said just before I walked away.

This is a first edition from
Audacity Books
Please visit us on the web at
www.audacitybooks.com
For information, please send your request to
info@audacitybooks.com.

This collection of short stories is the latest offering from Bruce K Beck and Audacity Books. It will soon be followed by the continuation of these characters' stories in **SPRING TALES**. Look for the **Holiday Novella Series**, which includes **GIVING THANKS, INDEPENDENCE DAZE, MY EASTER MIRACLE,** and **A BUCKSKIN CHRISTMAS**. They follow Bruce's **Tolerance Trilogy—SUCH A GOOD MAN, IT'S THEIR WAY,** and **THIS IS GOD'S COUNTRY**. Look for the **Obsession Trilogy—INK OBSESSED, OPERA OBSESSED,** and **LOVE OBSESSED**. And the **Love Trilogy: YOU'RE SURE TO FALL IN LOVE, LOVE AND THE EPIDEMIC**, plus **AND LOVE ENDURES**. For updates, and for occasional gifts and offers, please subscribe at:

www.audacitybooks.com/#subscribe

Many thanks to Walter Maas for his generous wisdom, and to Richard Kutner for his classy edits. Tim Barber of Dissect Designs (www.dissectdesigns.com) signed on as a cover designer for my first novel and then became a friend. You're Sure to Fall in Love, indeed. This journey would not have been possible without the example and the teaching of Joanna Penn at www.thecreativepenn.com. I am delighted, Joanna, to add this volume to your long list of books you have enabled. No doubt you will hit your one million mark any day now!

Bruce K Beck is both a writer and an accomplished chef. His novels—including the **Love Trilogy,** the **Obsession Trilogy**, and the **Tolerance Trilogy,** plus the **Holiday Novella Series**—are available online and wherever books are sold. Watch for Bruce's **Four Seasons Series** of short stories. Before turning to fiction, Beck authored ***PRODUCE: A FRUIT AND VEGETABLE LOVERS' GUIDE***, which was called "gorgeous" by ***The New York Times***, "a dazzler" by ***Bon Appetit***, and "the most spectacular food book of the year" by ***The Boston Globe***. His next book was ***THE OFFICIAL FULTON FISH MARKET COOKBOOK***, which was called "invaluable" by Jacques Pépin, and "a treasure" by Irene Sax of ***Newsday***. And Rex Reed said, "... you'll love this book. It's like a movie!"